DEATH BY CHOCOLATE

AN ADDIE FOSTER MYSTERY

KIMBERLEY O'MALLEY

This is a work of fiction. All names, characters, places, and events are a product of the author's very vivid imagination. Any resemblance to actual persons, events, or places is purely coincidental.

Published by Carolina Blue Publishing, LLC

ISBN: 978-1-946682-24-6

Created with Vellum

PRAISE FOR KIMBERLEY O'MALLEY

DEATH COMES IN THREES - ADDIE FOSTER BOOK 1

"This was my first cozy mystery and I have to say I absolutely loved it. Kimberley did an amazing job at keeping me guessing what was coming next. I can't wait to see what happens between Addy and Detective Wolfe cause something has to happen between them!

I also want to know who the man in Addy's dream is. And why those men were after her.

Can't wait for the next book!"

—Under Cover Book Blog

"This was the first Cozy Mystery and Kimberley knocked it out of the park. I loved Addie and Grey and the two aunties. The detective puts out the vibe he is serious and hard core. But I am sure he has a soft spot for Addie. Hopefully in the next book we will see where the sparks fly for Addy and why these guys were after her. KUDOS to Kimberley for such a great read."

—Wanda Bridget Hickey, Verified Kindle customer

"This was my first Cozy Mystery and I loved it. I was drawn in by Addie and adored Grey. He was such a charming, funny, and protective character. I can't wait to find out more in book two. This book is great for rainy days or a light read while you're on holiday."
—Author T. S. Petersen

DYEING FOR CHANGE - ADDIE FOSTER BOOK 2

"Love Addie mysteries, but hate that they are such a quick read. And that I have to wait for the next one!"
—Amazon certified customer.

"A cute, wacky, entertaining adventure! Another murder, more misadventures, and mayhem! A hot Detective, a soon to be ex, and right back in the middle of his investigation. Will she ever get a date?"
—A. Aguilar, Amazon certified customer

"I am really liking this series! A nice, easy, and quick read - just enough to take a break from real life and spend a lazy hour or so with a good read. Likeable characters and a continuing mysterious thread involving the main character throughout the two books so far - looking forward to seeing what happens in Book #3!"
—Vivian F. Shane, Amazon Kindle customer

MURDER BY NUMBERS - ADDIE FOSTER BOOK 3

"Murder by Numbers by Kimberley O'Malley is the third book in the author's Addie Foster Mystery series. This installment finds our beloved Addie still dealing with her bad dreams, and finding it difficult to avoid trouble. When her estate sale book purchase turns out to be more than she bargained for, she has to solve the mystery before she winds up toes up. This series is full of quirky characters, mystery, and plenty of fun reading."

—Dee, Words That Sparkle

"Wow if mystery is what you're looking for this book has it. This is the third book and Addie seems to find things that get her into trouble. She love estate sales and she found a book that she thought was very different. After purchasing this book she starts to get followed by this creepy English guy who turns out to want that book and is threatening all her family if he doesn't get it. The Author keep you looking for clues and wanting to know how this is going to end. It was an easy fun read."

—TX Shadow

ANGEL OF DEATH - ADDIE FOSTER BOOK 4

"I think this is my favorite Addie Foster book! Addie and Jonah are a cute couple. He's all alpha protective and she is bubbly and I know I shouldn't do this but I'm going to anyway when it comes to mysteries. Everyone needs a gay bff like Grey. He's someone who you can depend on to be there and will always make you laugh. I love the 2 aunts who worry about her aging eggs lol and of course the two smiling dogs. The suspense is great and laughs are plenty in this one."

—Carolyn, Verified Amazon Customer

"Addie, Grey and the aunts are on the road again. A friend of Addie's wants her to help find out what happened to the elderly man. With a stalker, it adds mystery to the story. The story was great with enough suspense to cause you to want to finish the book. Great read."

—R.W. Verified Amazon Customer

"Someone recommended the first book in the series yesterday, so I grabbed that one last night. At 3:30 this morning, I finished book 3! Loving this series, highly recommended!"

—Kindle Customer

To my readers for keeping me sane in this craziest of times.

Addie crept toward the door, back flattened against the outer wall. She hoped the dim light would keep her hidden. She shouldn't go farther. Knew this. But she went anyway. Something compelled her to look into the room. Cold beads of sweat trickled down her spine as she reached the partially opened door. Just a few more steps. If the coast were clear, she could peek inside. She inched along the wall another few feet, finally reaching the door. Heart pounding in her chest, Addie peered into the room. And gasped! A man's body, mostly obscured by an overturned table, lay still on the floor. Too still. Addie slipped farther into the room. Something about his shoes struck a chord. Leaning around the debris, she peered down into the man's face. Into Jonah's face...

"No!" Addie screamed. She fought against the hands holding her. She had to get away. She had to get help. Where was her phone? "Let me go!"

"Addie, honey, you're okay," came the most wonderful sound ever.

She stared at Jonah's face, drinking in the healthy color, the scruff of stubble on his jaw. Sobs broke from her, and she buried her face in his chest.

"Shhh, you're okay, I promise," he repeated over and over into her hair.

The weight of Jonah's hand stroking her back slowed her heartbeat. Gave her hope. Dispelled the lingering cobwebs of fear in her brain. Although she'd been having these "nightmares" for the better part of a year, today's by far ranked the worst. The memory of Jonah lying so still on the floor brought on another wave of tears.

"You have to promise me you'll be careful," she sobbed into his chest.

She felt him shift his weight on the bed before he gathered her in his arms, pulling her across his lap.

"I guess our break is over, huh?"

She nodded, still not quite ready or able to put words to the disturbing scene.

"I promise to do everything I can to come back to you. Every. Day."

The familiar words didn't carry their usual weight. Each time Jonah left for work, he whispered those same words to her. Even though Ocean Grove was a small beach town in North Carolina with a relatively low violent crime rate, being a detective carried more risk than the average career. Addie knew that when she met him. After all, Jonah was first on scene when she found a dead body. The *first* time it had happened.

And, normally, the words gave her comfort. But not today. Not after seeing him lying on the floor, deathly still, in her nightmare. She hugged him tighter, running her fingers over the muscles of his back, as though memorizing him.

If anything happens to him...because of me...

"Are you ready to tell me?" he asked.

Addie pulled back enough to see his face. His gorgeous, alive face. And nodded.

"You've probably already guessed I had a nightmare."

One corner of his mouth curled up. "We really need another word for them. 'Nightmare' doesn't really cover it."

"Agreed." *Especially this time.*

She struggled for a moment with whether or not to tell him. But she'd promised to always be honest with him, tell him the details. A sigh escaped her. Telling him had never been this tough before.

"Just tell me. I can already hear the gears turning in your head," he joked.

Addie gave him her best, albeit slightly watery smile. They relied upon humor in these times to keep them both sane.

"You know these, whatever we're calling them, aren't always clear. Or correct," she began. Addie took both his hands in hers. "I don't know where I was. Right now, that doesn't matter. The thing is…uh…the th-th-thing is..." She stopped when fresh tears rolled down her cheeks.

"Whatever it is, no matter how bad, we've got this. We always have in the past."

Addie sucked in the rest of her tears, wiping her eyes on the towel Jonah had slung over his shoulder before this all started.

He reached around her and into the drawer of the table on her side of the bed. She watched him grab the small notebook she kept in there. Taking the pen clipped to it, Jonah turned to a fresh page.

"Okay, I'm ready. Go ahead."

They'd started writing down every detail she could remember after waking. Sometimes even the tiniest thing counted. She took a deep breath and released it slowly.

"I walked into a dark, interior room. It looked like a fight had taken place. Or maybe a struggle. A table was overturned, and some chairs also. I smelled food, but I'm not sure what kind. Something sweet. And you."

Jonah looked up from where he was scribbling down her words. "Me?"

A new wave of hot tears burned her eyes, but she refused to cry. "You. Jonah, I found you lying on the floor. Not moving. I think you may have been d-d-dead."

*a*n hour later, Addie devoured the chocolate chip pancakes Jonah had made for breakfast. After dropping her bombshell, he'd urged her to take a long, hot shower and offered to make breakfast. She glanced at the debris littering her counters and sink. And couldn't care less. She loved Jonah, and he could make all the mess he wanted. The mess meant he was alive.

She speared a chunk of pineapple from the mixed fruit he'd dished up alongside the pancakes. The fact that he wanted her to be as healthy as possible brought a smile to her face.

"I love you, Jonah. I hope you know that."

The man in question smiled before taking her hand and kissing her palm. "I know, and I thank my lucky stars every day."

That sentiment squeezed her heart. "I'm not sure why. Being involved with me has only brought you danger and injury with a dash of terror thrown in."

Jonah squeezed her hand. "Better that than a life without you."

Her heart fluttered in her chest. "I'm the lucky one."

And she had been, they had been, for a few months. The crazy, prophetic nightmares had stopped after the last round at Thanksgiving. They'd celebrated their first Christmas together without the twin specters of danger and death hanging over them. In fact, the entire winter had passed without so much as a hint of anything. Even her stalker had remained silent. Although eerily so. They lived each day waiting for the other shoe to drop.

"No idea where this latest edition takes place?" Jonah asked as he scooped up another bite of breakfast.

"Not even one. But that's nothing new."

He glanced at the time on his phone. "I gotta go. Especially if I want to be home on time for tonight." He stood and took his plate to the sink.

"Tonight?" Addie asked.

Jonah turned, grinning at her. "Surely, you haven't forgotten our date. Our cooking date?" He came back to the table to kiss her. "I have to go. Are you sure you're all right?"

She stared at him for a moment before his words dawned on her. "Oh, right, Grey's gift. I may have forgotten."

"Yes, that cooking date," He came back to the table to kiss her. "I have to go. Are you sure you're okay?"

Addie nodded and watched him dash down the hall to their bedroom. Through the open door, she could hear the sound of him brushing his teeth and getting ready for work. She smiled.

Our bedroom.

Last month, Jonah placed his house on the market. Their realtor, Sue, had advised them spring is the hottest time for sales.

More importantly, Jonah had moved in with her...well, in with her and the girls. Addie glanced down at Gracey and Lily, her two Shetland Sheepdogs. The girls watched her every move, hoping in their little doggy hearts – and tummies – she'd drop something.

"Sorry, ladies, but chocolate is a no-no for you." She laughed at their expressions. At her words, both dogs turned their heads, as if actively listening. "I know, it's not a good idea for me either, but it's poison to you. No more emergency vet visits, please."

She shuddered at the thought of the last one, when a thug from New York had hurt her Gracey when the poor baby tried to protect Addie. Thankfully, her pup had only minor bruising. It could have been so much worse. As Jonah's gunshot wound the next day could have been. She shook her head to clear it of such thoughts.

"Are the girls trying to talk you into a treat?" Jonah asked on his way back into the kitchen.

Addie grinned at his back while he filled his travel mug with coffee. He also was a caffeine addict.

"Oh, they tried."

And then she groaned. "Do we really have to go to this cooking date?"

Jonah turned, openly laughing at her. "Yes, we do. Grey was so pleased with his little gift. You know he'd never let you forget if we blew it off."

"Tell me again why Grey is my oldest friend?"

"Because you two have that great love-hate thing going on. Well, not hate. More like getting under each other's skin."

"The annoying brother I never wanted," she said on a sigh. "But you're right, I do love him."

"And he's even grown on me," Jonah joked.

"True enough. You're my first boyfriend who's ever understood our relationship and not been threatened by it." She laughed at the frown on his face.

"His being gay helps." He swooped down to kiss her once more. "We also have to think of a better term for our relationship. Don't you think I'm a bit old for a 'girlfriend?'"

"'Significant other?' 'Better half?' 'Partner in crime?'" She laughed aloud. "Oh, I like that last one. And then there's 'lady friend,' 'lover,' 'paramour.'"

Jonah held up both hands, as if in surrender. "Let me think about that." A mysterious smile teased his lips. "Gotta go. See you after work."

Both girls followed him to the door, and he stopped to pat them on their silky heads before leaving. Addie sighed, watching him. An audible whine came from the door before the girls trotted back to her side. They sat and looked at her, as if reminding her to hurry.

"Yes, I know. It's almost time for work."

At that word, the dogs ran circles around the table, yipping and barking. That was life with a herding dog. Or two.

"All right, I know, I know. Give me a moment to get ready."

Addie rushed through her morning routine and left not long after Jonah. She made the short drive to Smiling Dog Books, her indie bookstore in town, with the windows partially down and the radio blasting. Nothing like a little Jimmy Buffett to get your blood pumping and put a smile on your face. The smile widened when she spotted Grey's car in the space next to hers behind the store.

"Uncle Grey beat us here. Let's go, girls!"

More yips from the back of the car let her know how the girls felt about that. Addie couldn't get to the hatch quick enough for them. She laughed as they pranced around, each trying to beat the other out of the car.

"Settle, please," she advised in her serious voice. That bought her a moment of peace while they held back their enthusiasm. "Much better. Out we go."

Addie grabbed both their leashes as they jumped out of the car. She had her hands full between two excited dogs in one and her purse and laptop bag in the other. She locked the car and made her way toward the back door, trying not to trip over the girls.

"Where have you been?" Grey's loud greeting was mostly drowned out by the girls barking when they spotted him.

"Hey, I'm the one who feeds you," she reminded them but smiled when he bent down to love on them.

"Not my fault they love their Uncle Grey more." He took the leashes from her hand and held open the door with a hip. Once inside, he unclipped both, and they dashed to their place behind the counter.

Addie muttered a noncommittal noise and followed the girls. "Since Jonah is all excited for our 'cooking date,' you might not be *my* favorite at the moment."

"Finally! I thought maybe you'd forgotten," he lamented, with his usual drama. "Again," he added, with a wink.

"Not likely, between you reminding me every other day and Jonah all excited about it."

For Valentine's Day, Grey had 'gifted' them a couples' cooking class with a local chef. Really his idea of a joke, but Jonah had been way more excited than Addie expected. Neither one of them cooked much, as evidenced by the large number of take-out menus in her kitchen junk drawer.

Despite her reluctance, the idea grew on Addie. And then came a round of violent stomach bug. On Valentine's Day, of course. First one in longer than she cared to remember that she actually had someone to celebrate with. The bug lasted two days, the only bright side being a loss of five pounds...and then Jonah got it. After surviving the "in sickness" part, Jonah moved into her house. He insisted his townhome was too much of a "bachelor pad" and worried about the girls losing their yard. If Addie hadn't already fallen head over heels for him, that would have tipped the scales.

Weeks passed, busy with his moving in, then placing the townhome on the market. Then one day Grey asked if she "ever intended to use his gift," in his usual snarky manner. Jonah, a fan of any food, chimed in, agreeing. And so, tonight was the night.

And it wasn't that she wasn't excited...well, mostly not that. But cooking, like a lot of domestic chores, fell by the wayside in her busy life. And the Aunties were all too happy to supply the couple with meals. Still, she should learn to make something other than breakfast and pasta.

She smiled, thinking about their class tonight. "Maybe this won't be so bad after all."

Grey planted a hand on one hip. "Wow, such enthusiasm. And after all the effort I put into your gift."

"And by 'effort,' you mean clicking a few keys on your laptop," she rebutted, with a grin.

"I used my phone."

Addie stuck her tongue out at him and joined the girls on the other side of the counter. She glanced around the small bookstore, her eyes flitting from rows of books to the small area with comfy furniture for people to sit and chat or read. She then grinned at her favorite area, the children's nook. She adored the little kids who came into the store, thirsty for a new story, another adventure. She held various story hours throughout the week and themed ones for holidays and seasons. Addie had become good friends with some of the young mothers.

All in all, Addie knew how lucky she was to be living her dream. When other little girls wanted to be teachers or veterinarians, she envisioned owning a bookstore. Just like this one. Because Smiling Dog was so much more. Sure, people came in for books, but they also came in to chat. To hang out in a peaceful place in this crazy world. And Smiling Dog was just the place for all of that, and more. The pastel colors and large windows that let in a flood of sunlight made for a calming atmosphere. Especially when she wasn't embroiled in a murder.

A FEW HOURS LATER, AFTER A ROUSING BUT SUCCESSFUL STORY hour, Addie sat on a stool behind the counter to catch a breath. Grey had taken the girls out to do their business before heading out to pick up their lunch. "A surprise," he'd called it before leaving. You never knew what that meant with him. This left her alone, except for a few customers, which she rarely got to enjoy.

With all the craziness since last summer, Jonah and Grey didn't like her being alone with customers. Especially since her stalker hadn't been identified. And though he – or she, for all Addie knew – had been quiet for a while, neither man wanted to risk her safety. And until this morning's latest entry in the Addie Foster Horror Show of Nightmares, she'd bucked them on it.

But now, with the terror of her vision still clinging to her like a damp sweater, Addie welcomed their overprotective-ness. Still, no matter where Grey went to grab their lunches, he wouldn't be more than a few minutes. Ocean Grove wasn't that big, and the summer crowd hadn't yet descended.

The bell over the door chimed, pulling Addie from her thoughts. She watched a tall, older man walk in, turning his head this way and that, as if taking in everything. She smothered a giggle, as she'd done the very same thing that morning.

He drifted away from her, down one row before doubling back and heading toward the counter.

"Good afternoon, and welcome to Smiling Dog Books," she greeted him. "Is there anything I can help you with?"

The man drew close enough for Addie to see the startling blue of his eyes, made more so by his jet black hair. Gray threading throughout only added to his look of sophistication. He wore black trousers, a white button-down shirt, and a dark charcoal blazer. Although she was far from a clotheshorse, Addie knew at a glance his were understated yet expensive. If only Grey was here. He'd know. Her best friend forever despaired about her lack of interest in that area.

The man stopped only when he came to the edge of the counter. His gaze was so intense, Addie felt as though it pierced her. And though she'd never seen this man before today, something seemed so familiar about him.

"Why, yes, I do need some help. I'm looking for Adelaide Foster," came his reply. His stare intensified. "Would you happen to be her?"

---

*a*ddie gripped the edge of the counter so hard, her skin whitened on her fingers. Her heart skipped a beat at his words, then thundered in her chest.

Of all times for Grey not to be here.

"I'm Addie Foster. Well, Adelaide, technically, but everyone calls me Addie." She forced herself to hold out her hand to him. "And you are...?"

The stranger shook her hand. She felt a buzz of sorts when he did. Not the kind of zing she got from Jonah. More of an awareness. Almost a familiarity. But that didn't make sense. He released her hand, and the buzz stopped.

"Forgive me. I am Robert Martin, and I was told to ask for you, Miss Foster." His voice held a faint trace of a British accent.

His blue eyes continued to mesmerize her. And then she remembered where she was. And who she was.

"Well, lucky you. Here I am. And how may I help you?"

"An...uh...associate of mine drove through Ocean Grove last summer. He raved about this place. Told me you had an extensive collection of local history books. I'm somewhat of a history buff. And now that I'm retiring soon, I'm thinking of relocating to the area."

Everything he said made perfect sense. Ocean Grove hosted tens of thousands of tourists every year. His friend, or associate, could very well have come through her store. And she did have a large local and North Carolina history section. But something felt off. Maybe his tone. Maybe the way he continued to stare at her, as if sizing her up. Maybe the nagging feeling that she knew him somehow. Whatever it was, the little hairs on the back of her neck didn't lie.

"Miss Foster?" he said, snapping Addie from her thoughts.

The bell over the door rang again, followed by Grey carrying take-out bags. Her knees weakened at the sight of him.

"Sorry. Your friend was right. We do carry many books about the area." She waved to Grey, rerouting him from taking their food to her office. "My associate, Grey, knows more about this subject than I could ever hope to. Grey, be a dear and show this gentleman to our local history section, please."

Something in her tone must have caught his attention. Grey stepped right up to the counter, placing the food next to her, and did as she asked, with his usual aplomb. He turned to face the stranger.

"Hi there. I'm Greyson Waverly, Addie's best friend and jack of all trades around here. But you may call me Grey. Now follow me."

Addie reached behind her for the stool, lowering herself to it as her legs threatened to give way. She kept her hands clasped in her lap to keep them from shaking. The girls, always so tuned in to her emotions, gathered around her feet. Lily whined in a low tone, while Gracey reached out and licked Addie's ankle.

She concentrated on her breathing for a moment, in and

out. Not wanting to bother Jonah, Lord knew she'd leaned on him many times in the past year, she resisted texting or calling him. Grey would come back in a moment and let her know what he thought. For as much of a joker as her best friend was, he had an uncanny ability to read people. Surely, if there was something wonky about Robert Martin, Grey would clue her in.

She focused on petting the girls until he returned, crooning softly to them with a confidence she didn't feel.

She was suddenly startled when Grey lounged across the counter directly in front of her.

"So? Who's the silver fox?" he asked.

"That may be the very last thing I expected from you," she told him.

He raised one blond brow. "Really? You know I've had a longer than average dry spell." He raked a hand through his perfect hair. "Well, at least for me." He then let out a dramatic sigh. "Sadly, I didn't get the vibe from him."

"Did you get any other vibe?"

"Like what kind? Because really, the whether-he's-gay-or-not-vibe is all that matters. At least to me."

"Grey! I meant more of the is-he-a-serial-killer vibe?" she whispered in return.

If she hadn't been so shaken by the encounter, Addie might have laughed at the widening of Grey's eyes.

"No, I don't believe Mr. Martin came here to kill anyone, if that's what you're asking."

"Considering our recent history, Grey, it wasn't that strange of a question."

Even though his words brought her a measure of comfort, her heart continued to pound in her chest. Addie glanced down the aisle where the stranger stood, reading the back of a book.

"Ah, honey, I'm sorry. You're right. You can't be too

careful these days, with everything that's happened." He came around the counter and wrapped an arm around her shoulders. "I've got you. But maybe Jonah was right. Maybe you shouldn't be in the shop alone."

She chose to ignore that. She'd deal with Jonah later.

"I'm just extra spooked because of the dream," she muttered. She then wished she could reel the words back into her mouth.

"What? Something you'd care to share with the class, Ms. Foster?"

Too late...

"I had another of those, whatever you want to call them this morning."

"Nightmare, bad dream, night terror, maybe prophecy…"

He stopped mid-sentence, probably around the time she felt the blood drain from her face.

"Please don't say prophecy," she whispered around the terror lodged in her throat. The memory of seeing Jonah like that… Addie shook all over, unable to get it under control. She turned into Grey's arms, willing the vision to stop playing in a loop in her head.

"Tell me what happened," he implored.

"Pardon me," came the voice again. The familiar yet not voice. "Are you quite well?"

Addie straightened up, backing from Grey's arms.

"Yes, of course." She put on her biggest smile, hoping to fool him. "Did you find what you were looking for?"

He lifted a book on Ocean Grove itself. One that told of local lore about ghosts, and even the buried treasure that had eluded Grey for months now. "I'll start with this one."

He handed it toward Addie, who took it to ring up, silently cursing the shaking of her hands.

"That'll be seventeen dollars and eleven cents, please."

He handed her a twenty.

Addie handed him the book in a complimentary reusable bag and his change. Before she could stop herself, she blurted out, "Do we know each other?"

Something she could not fathom flitted across his face. The impassive mask then slid into place.

"I don't believe so." He pocketed the change. "I'm staying in the area for a few days, maybe I'll see you again. Have a good day."

Addie mumbled the appropriate response, staring as he left the store. "There's something so…I don't know…familiar about him." She whirled to Grey. "Does he look familiar to you?"

"I wish! Did you see what he was wearing? Burberry jacket, unless I'm mistaken." He snorted out a laugh. "And I'm never mistaken about clothing."

A high-pitched laugh ripped from Addie. "I knew it! When he came in and I looked at what he was wearing, my first thought was you'd know what brand he wore." The laughter poured out of her until she had to bend over to catch her breath. Darn her terrible habit. The worse things got, the harder she laughed.

Grey pretended to inspect his nails. "Well, you would be correct. But that's hardly the point. Now spill!"

"Why don't we eat while I tell you?"

Addie took a minute to give each of the girls a bone to work on. She smiled as they went to the big, fluffy dog bed they shared. Anything to buy her a minute of silence. She needed to gather her thoughts and soothe her frazzled nerves.

Grey took their deli sandwiches from the bag; club for her, roast beef for him. He held up two bags of chips. Addie pointed to the sour cream and onion ones.

"As if you'd ever choose another type," Grey joked, ripping open his bag of barbecue chips.

"I'm willing to share," she offered.

Grey shook his head, then made a gesture for her to "spill."

Addie took a bite of her sandwich, then told him about the nightmare. Even hours later, dread wound its icy tendrils through her heart. No matter how sunny the day, no matter having Grey next to her, no matter Jonah texting her every hour, she couldn't shake the feeling of doom. Addie had never loved someone as she loved Jonah. And she couldn't lose him. Wouldn't lose him.

Grey put down his food and wrapped his muscular arms around her. "Nothing will happen to Jonah. I promise."

Addie sniffed back tears. "You can't make that promise." She leaned back to stare in his face. "We promised, pinky promised, really, years ago that we'd never lie to each other. That means not making promises we can't keep."

He nodded his eyes overly bright. "I will do everything in my power to keep my word."

She nodded since words wouldn't pass her heavy throat.

"Besides, you guys are relationship goals. Like John Krasinski and Emily Blount."

She laughed, hiccupped, and sobbed, all at the same time. "What would I ever do without you?"

"Wear Crocs in public?"

Laughter overtook her, as she knew had been his point. "I love my Crocs."

Grey shuddered. "I know. And yet I still love you."

They went back to eating their lunches. Customers came and went, and the rest of the day passed peacefully. And yet Addie couldn't shake the feeling that she had met Robert Martin, her mysterious customer, somewhere before.

That evening, Addie had finished putting in a pair of earrings when she heard the front door open and close. And then a chorus of doggy helloes.

Jonah!

She ran from their bedroom, eager to see him. Stopping at the edge of the living room, Addie took in the sight of him. His suit jacket was off and tossed on the back of a chair. His tie remained, but he'd loosened it. His dark hair bore tracks through it where he'd run his fingers at some point. Jonah was a sight for sore eyes.

Addie closed the distance, throwing herself into his outstretched arms. "You're here," she murmured into his chest.

"As I promised," he answered, his breath grazing the sensitive skin of her neck.

She sniffed in the scent of him, then stepped back a bit to drink in the sight of him. "I'm not crying," she informed him.

"Good. You know I hate it when you cry." He kissed her thoroughly but quickly. "Now, give me ten minutes for a quick shower, then we can go."

"Okay." Addie watched him grab his jacket and head down the short hall to their bedroom.

Knowing he would only take a short while – men had it so easy – Addie let the girls out to the back yard before feeding them dinner. The memory of her nightmare had stayed with her all day, and even now, hours later, the feeling of dread remained.

Still, this would be fun, she decided.

Shaking off her bad mood, Addie walked into the bedroom to grab a sweater to wear over her sleeveless black dress. She hadn't been sure how to dress, but her "dressy" choices were limited anyway. And everyone knew you couldn't go wrong with an LBD (something she learned from Grey).

Jonah turned to face her. "Are those your mother's earrings?"

Addie reached up to finger the ruby stones in her ears. "Yes. I have so few things of hers. The Aunties always said she loved this stone. They gave them to her for her college graduation. I figured a red stone would be a perfect choice for our make-up Valentine's date."

He closed the distance between them, leaning in to kiss her cheek. "Anything would have been great. You're so beautiful. But I'm glad they belonged to her. I wish I could have met her."

"She would have loved you. I was so young when she died, but I remember some advice she gave me. 'Never settle, Addie.' At the time, I wasn't sure what she meant." She kissed his cheek, stopping to wipe off a smudge of her lipstick. "But now, since meeting you, I get it."

"Keep saying stuff like that, and we won't get to our date," Jonah growled in her ear.

"You won't catch me complaining."

"Do you really not want to go?" Jonah asked. "We can order a pizza, but only if you wear that dress. You take my breath away."

Addie's heart gave a funny little beat, but she shook her head. "No, you've looked forward to this for weeks. And then there's Grey. Who wants to hear him whine again?"

"There is that. How about we go do this thing? And then, when we get home..." Jonah whispered something in her ear that brought a rush of color to her face.

4

They took her car, not his truck, in deference to the dress Addie wore. She'd tossed the keys to him when they headed out of the house. Leaning back in the passenger seat, she enjoyed being taken care of. Addie was as independent as women came. But she also knew a good thing when she had it. Over the past few months, she'd learned to share her life with Jonah. Reaching over, she curled her hand within his, giving it a squeeze.

He lifted their joined hands and kissed hers. "How was the rest of your day?"

"Well, no one died, so pretty good." She winced at her poor choice of words. "Sorry."

Jonah laughed. "No worries. If we can't joke about this, whatever this is, we might go crazy."

"Nice to know you don't already think I am. Crazy, I mean. After all, I'm the woman who has visions of scary things that frequently end in death."

He squeezed her hand. "This can't be easy for you. What can I do to help?"

"Not die?"

"Lucky for you, not in my plans for today."

"Ugh. I'm the worst. But ever since I started having these, whatever we're calling them, I've never had one that didn't come true. And since you're the 'star,' so to speak, I'm dreading whatever is coming."

"Understandable. Why don't we make a deal?" He turned his head and laughed at the expression on her face. "Tonight, we just focus on our date, relax, and have a good time. Tomorrow is time enough to figure out the latest of your whatever we decide to call them. How does that sound?"

"Perfect!" Addie replied on a sigh. *Why can't my life always be this simple?*

They chatted about their respective days until Jonah pulled into the parking lot of Café de Jardin. Addie flipped down the mirror to check her make-up. Since she rarely wore it, she always worried she wore too much. Or that she had lipstick on her teeth.

"You look amazing," Jonah commented. He grinned when she turned to face him. "And no, you don't have anything in your teeth. Although I'd be happy to ruin your lipstick." He waggled his dark brows.

"I'll hold you to that later. Let's do this." Addie waited until Jonah came to open her door, then she stood, smoothing her dress. "What do you think Chef Chevalier will be like? Grey raved about his food, which would not make Henri happy."

"Ocean Grove is a bit small for two French restaurants," Jonah joked.

"True. Shall we?"

Jonah grabbed her hand and led the way inside.

"You are late," snapped a tall, almost gaunt man in chef whites. The tall hat he wore moved as he shook his head.

Addie glanced at a clock on the wall. "Only a minute at most," she replied, biting her lip.

"And that is one minute I will never get back. This way." He turned on his heel and strode away, his spine as straight as a board.

"I guess we should follow him," Addie whispered.

"If not, we might be sent to the principal's office," Jonah joked in return.

"I do not have all night," the man snapped. He stood in the kitchen doorway, holding open the swinging door. "I assume you are no longer malade. Or sick, as you would say."

"What?" Addie asked before realizing what he meant. "Oh, no, of course not. That was in February. I just had a touch of the flu." She and Jonah followed the man into his kitchen.

"Or perhaps it was food poisoning from another, lesser French restaurant."

Addie tensed at his words. *Surely, he doesn't mean Le Bistro?* Chef Henri's restaurant had been here long before this place. She was about to say something when the man waved a hand.

"It is of no matter. I am Chef Guillaume Chevalier, and this is my restaurant. Your friend, Monsieur Waverly, made an excellent choice sending you to me."

He stopped, raking his eyes up and down both Addie and Jonah. She couldn't help feeling they had failed his inspection.

"Tell me about your experience with cooking French food, Mademoiselle Foster."

Addie glanced around the kitchen, realizing she'd never seen most of the instruments hanging, let alone used any of them. "I…uh…don't really cook."

The chef made a sound that didn't sound like it was in English, but his meaning wasn't missed. Even though Henri winced when she asked for mac and cheese rather than macaroni au fromage, he didn't insult her to her face. She would get Grey for this.

"Since I had no knowledge of your experience, I have

chosen a simple yet classic French dessert, Mousse Au Chocolat. Chocolate mousse to you." He waved a hand over the stainless steel counter. "I have laid out the necessary ingredients. Shall we start?"

"Do I get a hat like yours?" joked Jonah.

Addie smothered a laugh, loving him even more. Noah would have taken this man way too seriously. Yet another reason that relationship died early. Of course, Jonah was the actual cause of death.

"This is a toque blanche, not merely a hat," the chef muttered through clenched teeth. "If we could proceed?"

Addie choked back the urge to tell him where to put his toque blanche. Instead, she smiled her best, fakest smile and nodded.

"Bon! First, we gather the necessary ingredients." He waved one long, bony hand over the work area. "As you can see, I have already done so. Of course, you may not have these at home."

The look on his face told her everything she needed to know.

"Well, I usually just break out a Twinkie for dessert." She bit the inside of her mouth to keep from laughing at his look of horror. And because she couldn't help herself, Addie added, "However, if company is coming for supper, Jonah and I like to serve Rice Krispy treats; homemade, of course. Why, we even make special ones for the holidays, don't we, dumpling?" She batted her eyes at Jonah for effect. "But I suppose we could try making this pudding you're suggesting."

Jonah coughed but refrained from answering.

"Mon Dieu! Mousse Au Chocolat is *not* pudding. It is not even in the same room as pudding." Chef Guillaume's voice had taken on a shrill tone that only made her want to laugh.

"My apologies, Chef G. I certainly didn't mean to offend

you or the Mousse Au Chocolat." Addie deliberately mangled the last word, despite having taken four years of French between high school and college. The man deserved at least that. And if her southern accent had thickened ten-fold, oh well.

Chef Guillaume flushed an alarming shade of red, his face almost blending in with the scarf he wore around his neck. His fake smile rivaled her own. "Let us continue." He handed each of them a mixing bowl. "Watch carefully."

Addie ground her teeth but did as she was told. The chef broke several eggs, separating the whites from the yolks. He moved along at lightning speed, demonstrating how to melt the chocolate. By the time he whipped the egg whites into peaks, Addie wanted to scream.

What was Grey thinking?

She hated to cook and only excelled at ordering out. He knew that. And Jonah wasn't looking for a Donna Reed wannabe.

Grey forever joked about her lack of domesticity. But between the Aunties' cooking and her friend Gerti's baking, why did she need to learn? She knew the Aunties wouldn't be here forever; after all, their eighty-fifth birthdays loomed. But she wanted to learn their recipes, make their meals. Because they cooked with love, not disdain, as this pompous chef clearly did.

She must have fumed for a while, as the chef had stopped speaking and turned to the large stainless steel fridge. He reached in and pulled out a tray with several dishes of completed Mousse Au Chocolat.

"As you can see, presentation is everything."

A mint leaf and fresh raspberries topped each dish. Despite her dislike of the man, Addie's stomach growled in appreciation. Dessert made her happy. Always. Their not eating before arriving didn't help. Grey had told them this would include dinner. Obviously not.

"Wow! That looks amazing," she said.

"Good enough to eat," Jonah agreed, earning a look from the chef.

The chef grabbed a spoon and took a taste of one of the cups of dessert. He closed his eyes while swallowing, making the oddest noises. Addie shifted her weight from one foot to the other. If they hurried, they could catch a late dinner at the diner. She snuck a peek at Jonah, hoping he could suddenly read her mind.

Let's go! I'm hungry...

Sadly, he didn't grab her hand and pull her out, promising never to subject her to French food again. Although she loved Henri's bistro. From now on, Henri would be her only French chef.

Chef Guillaume shoveled a few more spoonfuls of the mousse into his mouth before putting the dish on the counter. He then handed Addie a piece of paper. "I have written the instructions with a recipe. Not mine, of course, as that is secret."

"Of course," she demurred. Addie took the paper, hoping this signaled the end of her misery. "We cannot thank you enough, Chef, for taking time out of your busy schedule."

"Yes, yes," he muttered, a hand pressed to his head. "Your friend Grey has a way of influencing people, does he not?"

Jonah shuffled his feet. "Well, this has certainly been enlightening. Thank you, Chef." He held out his hand to shake the other man's. When the chef didn't respond, Jonah placed it on the small of Addie's back. "Well, we can see ourselves out."

They turned and left without another word from the chef. By the time they reached the sanctity of her car, Addie felt ready to pop.

"Can you believe that man? What a jerk! You, of course, could not understand the complexity of French delicacies," she growled in an over-the-top fake accent. "You are peasants, and I spit on you."

Jonah laughed until he had to wipe his eyes. "You have a terrible French accent."

He started the car and drove toward the town square. When he made a left onto Cottage Lane, Addie gasped.

"Did you read my mind?" she asked as he pulled in front of the diner.

"No, but I know you, Addie Foster. We didn't eat before that disaster. And your stomach could be heard in Wilmington when he brought out the 'pudding.' Two cheeseburgers with sweet potato fries to go, coming up." He leaned in and kissed her. "I may have texted Otto before we left. Be right back."

Addie sighed and sat back. Even though tonight's adventure turned out to be an epic failure – and she would have a chat with Grey about this – she was going home with the man she loved. And Otto's sweet potato fries. What more could she want?

She reached down to grab her purse. She wanted to text Grey, give him a head's up to the amount of trouble he was in, when she realized she'd left her purse at the café.

Great! Now we'll have to deal with that jerk again.

Addie sat there, fuming, while she waited for Jonah. Of all the bad luck! Well, at least they had some of Gertie's berry pie in the fridge. It may not be French, but it was made with love and delicious to boot.

Jonah placed their takeout in the back of her car before getting in. "Yes, I got ranch for dipping," he said while starting her car. "Although I find the combination hideous, I know you don't."

Addie squeezed his hand. "Aren't you the best boyfriend ever?"

"Why, yes, I am," he joked before pulling away from the curb.

"Well, you're going to be an even better one when you don't grumble after I tell you something."

"I can only imagine. Go ahead."

"I may have left my purse back there."

"At Chef Jerk's?"

Addie laughed. "That's another point in your favor, but yes, at the restaurant.'

Jonah sighed. "Oh well, I guess I can wait another few minutes for Otto's heart attack burger."

"Not to mention his world famous sweet potato fries, dipped in ranch dressing."

Jonah shuddered. "I like to pretend you don't ruin them that way. I'll stick with the cinnamon butter, thanks."

"To each his own. Even if mine is way better," she joked.

"We'll have to poll your family. See what they think."

"The Aunties may side with you," Addie admitted. "But that's only because you're so cute."

"Not to mention I'm in a position to do something about your aging eggs," he quipped.

"I wish everyone would leave my eggs out of their daily conversations."

Jonah snickered. "They only do it because they care."

"Ha! The Aunties want a baby to hold and spoil. And don't you laugh. They won't stop with one. They'll want a whole passel 'before they die,' as they so like to remind me."

"I'm okay with that. I'm not getting any younger. We could start practicing; right after Otto's burger."

"Watch it, mister," she warned. "A girl might start taking you seriously."

Jonah pulled into a parking space at the side of the café. He turned to face her. "A girl should," he murmured.

Addie smiled at him, knowing her heart shined in her eyes. And not caring. When he said things like that, she believed in a future. Even the terrible nightmare lost its grip in the wave of love she felt for him.

The shrill ringing of his phone shattered the moment. She knew that ringtone. Jonah had picked the most obnoxious one possible for Dan, his partner. Not a fan of his, Addie took off her seatbelt.

"You answer that. I'll be right back."

"Wait, I'll come with you," he countered.

But she'd already gotten out of the car. "No, really. Take the call then shut off the phone. We have Otto's cooking and 'practice' to look forward to." She walked away with an exaggerated swing of her hips.

Addie pulled open the door of the café, a bit surprised the chef hadn't locked it yet. She made her way through the darkened restaurant until reaching the swinging door that separated it from the kitchen. Something made her hesitate. She stood there, hand on the door, goosebumps on her skin.

"Chef?" she called out.

A flash of that morning's vision teased her brain as she glanced around the interior. With only moonlight seeping through, the tables and bar became distorted, shadowed forms. Maybe she should have had Jonah come in with her.

Shaking off her silliness, Addie straightened her spine and resolve.

Just open the door and grab your purse.

She did just that, swinging the door inward and entering the kitchen. The overhead lights made her blink after having to squint in the murky outer room. Spying her purse on the counter, Addie grabbed it, but when she turned to leave, she spied the chef lying on the floor. Several mixing bowls and cooking instruments lay strewn around him.

"Chef?" she called again her voice tremulous this time. Addie crept to where he lay, too still, on the floor. Cold sweat trickled down her spine. She crouched next to him. "Chef Guillaume?" she tried once more. Nothing. She peered closer. When he didn't seem to be breathing, Addie ran from the room.

She stumbled through the darkened restaurant area, banging her leg against a table. Crying out, she didn't stop as she ran for the door. Just as she barreled through it, Jonah reached for her.

"Addie? What's wrong?"

She turned, pointing back at the restaurant. "In th-th-there. He's d-d-dead," she cried before collapsing in his arms.

5

The warmth and strength of Jonah's arms were all that kept Addie from giving in to the darkness that edged her vision. Burying her face in his chest, she blurted out what she'd found. His lips in her hair brought her a tiny sense of peace in this madness.

"I've got you," he murmured. "Give me a minute to get some help here."

She felt him take out his phone, then the low rumble of his voice filled the air. Addie squeezed her eyes shut and thought about her breathing. In. Out. Her knees trembled, but she held on to him with all her might.

I will not fall apart.

"I need to go inside, Addie. I want you to sit in the car and keep the door locked."

She shook her head, whimpering a protest, even though she knew he was right.

"Please, honey. I have to know you're safe."

She let him lead her to her car without protest. When she tucked herself into the passenger seat, Jonah leaned in and kissed her.

"I'll be right back. Lock this door, and do not open it for anyone. If anything happens, lay on the horn."

She nodded, words impossible past the lump in her throat, and watched him walk back toward the front of the restaurant. When he was out of sight, she hit the preset for Grey on her phone and waited.

"Well, was it everything you hoped? Wasn't Chef Guillaume fabulous?" Grey intoned over the phone.

"Chef is d-d-ead," Addie sobbed, hot tears spilling down her cheeks.

Silence reigned for a few moments. Then Grey made a choking noise.

"Even your cooking isn't that bad, honey."

A loud noise, half-laugh, half-sob, came from her throat. "Not funny. It'll be quite a while, if ever, before this is funny. He. Is. Dead."

"Maybe he's just pining for the fjords," Grey joked, quoting one of their favorite Monty Python skits.

"The man is dead. On the floor of his kitchen." Addie told him about their evening and then heading back in to retrieve her purse and finding his body on the floor.

"I'm on my way!" Grey yelled.

She heard a rustle, then the sound of his keys jangling. She sent a silent prayer to the universe in thanksgiving for such a friend.

"Hurry," she whispered. "Jonah had to do his cop thing. He went in there." And then the familiar feeling of dread crept down her spine. "I have to go."

With the memory of her nightmare fresh in her mind, Addie bolted from the relative safety of her car. Without any kind of plan, she ran into the restaurant, screaming his name. When he didn't answer right away, cold sweat slid down her spine.

"Addie, what's wrong?" Jonah yelled as he rushed from the kitchen.

She met him at the swinging doors, leaping into his arms.

"I was so scared for you. The dream, Jonah, the dream. This might be the place." She whipped her head around, trying to get a better look at the interior. But the low lighting from the kitchen hid more than it showed. She bit down on her bottom lip. "I don't know. The first nightmare is never specific."

"Hey, I'm right here, Addie." He pulled her head against his chest, cradling her. "I'm fine, and so are you."

She drew in a breath, breathing in his scent. It calmed her. The thunder of his heartbeat under her ear gave her strength and courage. Addie straightened up, then leaned back to see him better in the shadows.

"You're fine," she breathed.

Jonah grinned down into her face. His eyebrow, the one she loved with the scar dissecting it, raised. "You know I am," he joked.

"You knew what I meant," she protested.

Anything else she planned to say was stopped by the sounds of sirens and then running feet and voices. Many voices. One of which belonged to her best friend.

"Sir, this is a crime scene. You can't go in there," came a very masculine, and annoyed, voice.

"Gee, I can't imagine who that could be," drawled Jonah.

"I, uh, might have called him when I was in the car," Addie admitted. "Why don't I go wait outside with Grey?"

"Good idea. Please stop him from doing anything, well, Grey like." Jonah leaned down and kissed her on the mouth. "I'm sorry you were frightened. I'm fine. And I love that you care so much about me. Now let me do my thing."

"Of course," she murmured before turning toward the front door.

Addie pushed through it, at once blinded by the sea of light coming from the emergency vehicles.

"There you are," came a too familiar voice from her right. "Please tell this *gentleman* that I'm with you."

Addie walked up to the younger man dressed in a cop uniform. "Honestly, sir, I've never seen him before in my life," she joked, with a very straight face.

"Adelaide Foster, that is so not funny," cried Grey.

"It kind of is." She shook her head. "Sorry, Officer. I get a little goofy when I'm stressed. Detective Wolfe is my boyfriend. He and I were here tonight for a cooking lesson. I found the, uh, body. Jonah is inside."

"Yes, ma'am."

She grabbed Grey by the arm. "We should probably get out of their way," she advised, steering him toward the side of the restaurant, where her car sat in the parking lot. "Jonah will know where to find me."

Addie looked back when she felt a hand on her arm.

"I'm sorry, ma'am, but you can't leave. A lot of people are going to want to talk to you seeing as how you found the body and all."

It might have been her overly wild imagination, but the officer didn't look quite so friendly anymore. She gulped.

"Of course," she agreed. Addie glanced around herself and spotted a small wrought iron table and chairs in front of the restaurant. She grabbed Grey by the elbow. "We'll just be over here when they're ready to grill me."

The officer had the decency to flush before turning away. Addie lowered her tired body to a chair, then placed her head in her hands and moaned. "How is this happening? Again?"

"Must be that amazing Foster luck rearing its ugly head," joked Grey as he joined her.

She raised her head and looked at him. "All we wanted was date night. Is that too much to ask?"

"Oh, honey," Grey murmured, taking her very cold hands in his. "So tell me about Chef Guillaume. At least before he died."

Addie bit back a laugh. "I didn't figure out until partway through the lesson this was your idea of a joke." She shook her finger at him in her best angry schoolteacher look. "That man was rude!" Addie slapped a hand over her mouth. "Not to speak ill of the dead," she whispered through her fingers.

Grey howled across the table from her. He only reined himself in after a few questioning glances from nearby police.

"I'm so sorry, really. But the man could cook. And I figured you could use a little help in that area. Especially now since you and Jonah shacked up."

Addie glared a gesture completely lost on him, as usual. "Really, Grey? 'Shacked up?' That's the best you could do?"

"Do you prefer 'living in sin?'" he asked.

"Grey, right now, my living 'in sin' with Jonah is the least of my worries."

"You're right, of course. I'd be way more worried about how many pairs of baby booties the Aunties have knitted."

She counted to ten in her head, but he had a point. Already concerned about Addie's 'aging eggs,' her elderly maiden aunts, Beatrice and Clementine, had been over the moon when Jonah moved in. They'd started giving Addie advice-the kind one never wished to receive from family. But those were her Aunties, and she loved them. Even if they insisted on discussing ways Jonah could protect his sperm count...

"Guess how many teaspoons there are in a gallon."

"Huh?" Addie stared at Grey, wondering what she'd missed.

"Seven hundred and sixty-eight." Grey waved a hand in

front of her face. "Are you still there? Just checking to see if you're paying attention."

"I'm here." She looked around, grimacing. "Although I'd rather be just about anywhere else."

Grey cocked his head, a thoughtful expression on his handsome face. Thoughtful but devilish. She shuddered to think about the wheels turning in there.

"How about back at Tiffany's, dumping Noah?"

A giggle escaped her. "No, but that's a close second to this fresh Hell."

"What do you think happened to the chef?" asked Grey.

"I have no idea. He seemed fine when Jonah and I were with him. Well, if you discount the haughty nastiness. But healthy, you know? I mean, we'd only been gone maybe fifteen minutes."

"Hey," called Jonah as he strode toward them. He took Addie in his arms. "How are you holding up?"

"Fine, thanks for asking," Grey answered, tongue firmly in cheek.

"Did you just find a dead body?" Jonah snapped back.

"Boys!" Addie stepped out of Jonah's arms. "Then he's dead? Really dead? I couldn't see him breathing, but I wasn't sure…"

Jonah nodded. "He's really dead."

"Oh, I had hoped…" She sat down with a thud. "You would think I was used to seeing dead bodies." She shuddered. "Not sure I ever will be."

"It's not something you get used to. Trust me."

His grim tone brought her gaze to his face. Even though the situation was far from frivolous, something in his eyes sent a new wave of chills down her spine.

"What is it, Jonah?" she asked in a whisper.

Grey turned his head from her to Jonah, then back to her. He looked as though he was watching a tennis match. "How do you do that, Addie? How do you know something is wrong? I mean, other than Chef being dead and all."

"He didn't die of natural causes," Jonah muttered.

Addie stood so fast she lost her balance. "What? How do you know?"

Jonah didn't say anything at first. She could see the internal struggle. His being a detective meant he walked a fine line with what he could tell her. He opened his mouth to say something when a man cleared his throat behind Jonah.

"Detective Wolfe, a moment please." The white-haired man turned to Addie.

"Chief Winters, nice to see you again, sir," Addie babbled. "Well, not here of course. And not under these circumstances. You know what I mean. I'll shut up now."

Not only was Chief Winters the chief of police, which made him Jonah's boss, she'd also first met him when a gunman broke into Addie's home, intent on killing her. Jonah had shot the man dead right outside her bedroom door.

"And you, Miss Foster. And yes, the circumstances could be better." He nodded to her, always very professional but a little on the stiff side.

She shot Grey a look when he attempted to smother a laugh with a fake cough. Typical.

The chief nodded to another officer who joined their group. "Officer Burke, could you please escort Miss Foster to the station?"

"Yes, sir, of course." She turned to Addie. "If you don't mind, Miss Foster."

"No, of course not, Natalie."

Addie turned to Grey. "Could you take care of the girls, please? Maybe take them to the Aunties." The thought of her elderly aunts finding this out tonight turned her stomach even more. "On second thought..."

"Go, Addie. I've got this. I'll just bring the little darlings home with me." He stepped in, giving her a kiss on the cheek. "Don't worry, they'll be fine. You take care of you."

She hugged him. "Thank you, I will." Addie took a last, fleeting look at Jonah before turning to Officer Burke. "I'm ready."

She followed the other female, head held high. Once again, she'd found herself in a mess with the police.

Why is this happening again?

Officer Burke stopped next to a squad car. She smiled at Addie before dropping her gaze. "I'm sorry, but I have to ask you to sit in the back. You understand," she said, or maybe pleaded.

Addie nodded and got in the back. She understood, all right. Through no fault of her own, she was once again headed to the police department. Only this time, she seemed to be their number one suspect, rather than the victim of a violent crime.

6

"*I*'m not sure what else I can tell you, Dan," Addie muttered through clenched teeth. She wanted to pound her fists on the table, but the smug detective might get too much satisfaction from that. She'd repeated her story several times from start to finish, both to him and the police chief. At least she respected Chief Wells.

"Considering the circumstances, let's make it Detective Blackwell, shall we?"

His tone left no doubt he expected to be obeyed. She wanted to kick his shins. Or worse. Instead, she plastered yet another fake smile, number fifty-seven thousand of the evening, on her face and nodded. Addie didn't trust herself to speak. She'd never liked this man, in fact only tolerated him because he was Jonah's partner. Now she loathed him and his smugness.

"Nothing else to say, then, Addie?"

She gripped the edge of the table until her fingers turned white.

"It's Ms. Foster, and I would like my lawyer now. Please."

His eyebrows met his hairline. "Now, Addie, there's no reason for that. We're just having a friendly chat."

His clenched jaw belied his words. Addie resisted chuckling. Barely.

"There is nothing 'friendly' about tonight. And you have treated me like a suspect, Detective. So, unless you plan on charging me with something, I'll be leaving now."

Addie stood on shaking knees but stared him down. He got up slowly, making his way to the door. "Just don't go far," he warned, like the lead in a low budget film.

Addie swept by him, shaking now from rage more than fear. She passed through the big, open room, ignoring the stares and not-so-hushed talk. She didn't slow down until she reached the outer lobby. And Grey.

His scruffy face never looked so good. Addie threw herself into his open arms. "Thank you," she murmured into his chest.

"Where else would I be? I took the girls to my place and came right back." Grey leaned back to look into her eyes. "Are you okay?"

"Yes, but no thanks to that jerk. I swear, how can Jonah even be partners with him?"

"Maybe because they're the only two in this tiny department," he suggested. "Oh, I have to ask. Did someone named Big Bertha make you their…" He stopped midsentence at the look on her face. Then shrugged. "Too soon, huh?"

Addie held up her thumb and pointer finger, without any room between them. "Can we go, please?"

"What about lover boy?"

"I have no idea how long he'll be here. I'm not even sure where he is or what he's doing. They wouldn't let me see him." She waved her phone at him. "I'll text him that I'm going home."

"Okay, then let's blow this popsicle stand." Grey grinned. "I've always wanted to say that."

Addie rolled her eyes but followed him out the door. "It's a good thing you have a key to my house. I don't even have that. Jonah has my keys."

"Why don't we stop by and get the girls, then I can take you all home?" Grey suggested.

"Yes, please."

A few moments later, Addie rested her head against the seat and closed her eyes. Because it was spring in North Carolina, her allergy/sinus headache raged. Add to that the stress of the last few hours, and she was done. She crossed her fingers that Grey would take a hint.

"So, what's our plan?"

No such luck...

"What plan would that be?" she asked, without opening her eyes. Best not to engage fully.

"Tsk tsk, like I'm going to fall for that. First you have a nightmare, then you find a dead body. You must have a plan. You always have a plan. And a role for me to play."

She didn't have to open her eyes to know he was grinning. Sadly, he wasn't wrong. Well, she didn't have a plan. Yet. But she needed one and fast. Addie sighed.

"I'll let you know tomorrow when I think of something. Right now, I'm either having a stroke or just a really bad headache. Thinking hurts."

She felt him place a hand on her shoulder. And she remembered why she loved him so much, despite everything that came along with being best friends with Greyson Waverly.

Addie must have fallen asleep. The sound of an excited dog – well, two excited dogs – from the back seat woke her. She opened her eyes and reached around to pet two silky heads. "Hello, girls. Let's go home."

Both dogs licked her hand. She closed her eyes for the short trip to her house. The next time she opened them, she spotted her car and Jonah's truck in her, their, driveway. The front door opened before she was fully out of the car. The girls raced to greet Jonah, leashes dragging through the grass.

"Thanks again, Grey. I'll see you tomorrow." She waved as he got back in his car.

A text alert sounded from her phone. Addie glanced down. It was from Grey.

"Can't wait to get started on you know what..." A winking emoji followed. Addie groaned, turned off her ringer, and turned back to the house.

Jonah rushed to greet her, folding her in his arms while the girls danced around them, both getting tangled in their leashes. She stood there for a moment, ignoring the throbbing in her head, and merely soaked in his solid warmth. For someone who'd been in her life for less than a year, Addie had no idea what she'd do without him. The thought brought on more pain, so she blocked it out. Slipping from his arms, she looked into his handsome face.

"He may be your partner, but Dan Blackwell is a jerk. I'm through being nice to him." She grabbed the leashes and went inside.

"Tell me everything," Jonah urged. "And for the record, I know he's a jerk. He's not so much my partner as a co-worker, and I avoid him whenever possible." He kissed the top of her head. "Now tell me what he did."

She felt the tension begin to seep from her bones. "He did his job but enjoyed it a bit too much."

They took a seat on the couch while Addie told him everything, including Dan's terrible attitude. Jonah's very expressive face darkened as she spoke, so Addie rubbed one hand up and down his arm. Despite that, anger rippled off him in waves.

"He and I are going to have a little chat when this is all over," he grated between clenched jaws.

"He's not worth it, Jonah. What can you tell me about Chef?" Addie rubbed at her temples, willing away the pain.

Jonah's face softened. "There's nothing I can tell you right now. Autopsy is scheduled for the morning." He stood, then reached down a hand for her. "Let's get you to bed. I can see you're hurting."

Addie's heart warmed. She was a lucky girl. She reached up and kissed his cheek. "Can you take care of the girls?"

"Of course. I'll see you in a moment."

She gave him the best smile she could and headed to the bedroom. As she rounded a corner, she heard the big, tough detective praising the girls in the voice he used only for them. And her smile felt real for the first time that night.

Sunlight filtered through the blinds, awakening Addie from a deep, and thankfully nightmare-free, sleep. She stretched and yawned before noticing she was alone in the room. She then heard the murmur of several voices beyond her closed bedroom door. After using the bathroom, Addie walked down the short hallway to the kitchen. She paused at the entry, staring at the crowd of people gathered there.

"There's Sleeping Beauty," Grey joked. He popped a bit of bacon in his mouth, causing her stomach to rumble.

"Come in, dear. You must be starving," cooed her Aunt Beatrice. The elderly woman engulfed Addie in her arms and a cloud of lavender. She'd never subscribed to the notion of less is more. "Jonah told us you hadn't eaten dinner last night. Poor thing! You'll just waste away if you keep that up."

"I'm hardly in danger of that," Addie exclaimed. "But I won't say no to breakfast." She slid into a chair next to Jonah, who handed her a full plate. Her eyes bulged at the amount of food. "Goodness, Jonah, I missed one meal, not ten."

"Maybe she's eating for two," Clementine cackled.

Grey raised one eyebrow, staring at her. "No, I don't think so. Her face doesn't look any fuller," he mumbled around a mouthful of food.

"Neither do her..." Clementine added, waving a hand in the general area of Addie's chest.

She crossed her arms over her chest, glaring as everyone cracked up. Well, everyone except Jonah.

"Addie and I will be married first. I'm old-fashioned that way," he murmured, staring into her eyes.

His words set the butterflies to flight in her belly. Words escaped her, so she took a bite of her scrambled eggs.

Clementine cleared her throat. "Well, now that that's out of the way, who's going to tell me what happened to Chef Guillaume last night?"

Addie chewed and swallowed, trying not to choke. *How do they know already?*

"Uh...I don't know, Aunt Clementine. Maybe you should ask a detective," she suggested, smirking at Jonah.

Without missing a beat, Jonah said, "As you well know, I am not at liberty to say." He went back to eating his toast.

Clementine harrumphed.

"What's the advantage to having a detective in the family if he won't tell us anything?" Beatrice complained.

Glancing at the wall clock, Addie gasped. "Who let me sleep this late?"

Jonah and Grey both raised their hands, causing the Aunties to laugh.

"After the night you had, I figured sleeping in one morning wouldn't hurt," Jonah explained.

"And Erin came in early to open the bookstore," Grey added with a smirk. "The world can go on without you."

She stuck out her tongue at him and ate her breakfast.

When they'd all finished, the Aunties left for their weekly hair appointment. Those colors didn't come in nature after all.

Grey headed out right after them. "See you at the store soon, Boss."

Jonah shook his head. "They're like a tornado."

"Yes, they really are," Addie agreed. "But they're my tornado."

"Ours," Jonah corrected. He stood and gathered his dishes.

"I've got this. You cooked," Addie said. "Just need another cup of coffee first." She needed much more than that to get through this latest disaster but kept that thought to herself.

"Thanks. I'm going to get ready for work. Today should be interesting."

She watched him leave the room and sighed.

Why does he put up with me?

How normal Jonah's life must have been prior to her bursting into it. Then again, her own life had been pretty normal, boring even by other people's standards, before the visions and dead bodies started popping up.

Addie frowned into her coffee mug, trying to remember how her life was before all that. It seemed like a decade ago. She stood there, with the girls dashing about, noses in the air, and tried to remember life before all *this* had started. She still stood there when Jonah reappeared.

"Hey, no frowns," Jonah joked. Stopping long enough to give her a smacking kiss, he grabbed a travel mug and filled it with coffee. "This is not your fault, Addie. And you are not a suspect. I'll be having a little chat with Dan this morning."

"I know it's not my fault, but I'm getting tired of the dead bodies piling up around me." She bit her bottom lip to quell the tremble in it. "Tell me the truth. Don't you ever regret getting mixed up in all this?"

Jonah set down his coffee before pulling her toward him. He didn't say anything until she raised her eyes to meet his. "I love you, Adelaide Foster, with or without the craziness that surrounds you. I don't regret a thing. I love these sweet little dogs of yours. I love your...uh...interesting aunties. Even when they discuss my sperm count as if I'm not in the room."

Addie winced, then smothered a sound that was half-laugh, half-sob.

"Heck, I even tolerate Grey." He kissed her once more. "So no, I don't regret getting 'mixed up' with you. And now, I have to go. I have some butt to kick."

"Now that's something I can get behind. Have a good day. And stay safe."

"Always. Same goes for you." He waved before leaving through the front door.

Addie sighed, wondering once again how she'd gotten so lucky. She took care of the dishes before giving the girls their breakfast.

"We'll go to work once Mommy gets ready," she told them. "After all, I have a murder to solve."

7

"*E*rin, can I bring you back anything for lunch?" Addie asked as she grabbed her purse from her office.

She'd waited until Grey had to leave for a meeting at the Waverly Foundation. Since his parents were currently sailing around the world, and Harper, his older brother, lived in Europe, that left Grey to see to the family foundation. The Waverlys had money, and a lot of it. Neither son had shown any interest in the agricultural business founded by Grey's great-grandfather. Grey's grandfather, Josiah, had turned farming into a huge, profitable business. Grey's father, Sam, had tripled the profits. When Sam had sold the business for a ridiculous sum, the family had started a charitable foundation that gave money to everything from cancer research to underprivileged children.

Addie patted the girls and gave them each a bone to chew behind the desk. "Be good girls for Auntie Erin," she told them before heading for the door.

"I brought something, Addie, but thanks," said Erin, her part-time helper. She smiled and turned back to assisting a customer.

"Okay, I won't be long."

Once outside, Addie chose to walk the few blocks to Le Bistro, the French restaurant off the town square. Until recently, it had been the *only* French restaurant in their small town. She wondered if the Café du Jardin had put a dent in Henri's business. The thought made her sad.

How does Jonah do this all day?

She didn't want to think someone she knew could murder another human being, even one as snippy and rude as Chef Guillaume. If so, would competition be reason enough to kill? Shaking her head, Addie walked along, enjoying the sunshine on her skin. Chef Henri might be a bit over-the-top French and a food snob, but he wasn't a killer. She shook her head. She would pick up something to go, and if she had the opportunity to ask him a few general questions, so be it.

Turning the corner onto Maple Street, Addie walked around the town square instead of cutting through it. Every step counted! The extra few moments also gave her time to come up with a plan. Despite Grey insisting she always had one, she rarely did. Addie was more of a "seat of her pants" kind of girl. It had worked so far.

The early May sun suddenly lost its warmth. Addie looked up to see if clouds blocked it, but only a Carolina blue sky met her gaze. Yet she felt chilled. And then the tiny hairs at the back of her neck stood up. Not wanting to be obvious, she slipped on a pair of sunglasses before glancing in all directions.

Is someone watching me?

People walked in and out of the shops around her. Two young mothers sat on a blanket in the square, a pair of chubby toddlers between them. A man threw a frisbee to a border collie.

Nothing looked out of place, yet Addie couldn't shake the sudden feeling of danger. Of someone watching her. She quickened her steps, anxious to reach the safety of Le Bistro and tried not to cry. For months, her stalker had fallen silent; not an oversized bear or threatening letter in sight. And now, even though she hadn't heard from him – or her – again, Addie felt their eyes upon her. She sniffed back the tears and straightened her spine. Ocean Grove was her town. Nothing and no one would spoil it for her.

She should probably call or text Jonah. But what would she say? She had a bad feeling? She felt like she was being watched? No! She could do this.

Taking some deep breaths, Addie slowed her pace and tried to do the same with her heart rate. The few tables in front of Le Bistro held lunchtime diners, a sight that made her happy.

Addie walked in, stopping to slide her shades to the top of her head. She asked the young woman manning the door for a lunch menu. Standing off to the side, she perused the menu. Addie decided on the Salade De Poulet Aux Amandes. She gave the young woman her name and order before taking a seat at the small bar to wait.

She glanced around. Most of the tables held diners, so business seemed good. She eavesdropped on the ones closest to her, anxious to hear any talk of the other chef's murder. But no one seemed to know about it or care enough to discuss it.

Addie accepted a glass of ice water from the bartender and thought about the murder. Who would want Chef Guillaume dead? He was relatively new in town, opening his restaurant a few months ago. She hadn't heard anything about him other than speculation about the need, or not, for another French restaurant. She thought back to Gwen – or

Diana, as her name turned out to be. Her hairdresser had been murdered last year when trouble from her former life in New York City followed her to sleepy Ocean Grove. Maybe Chef Guillaume had similar circumstances?

Addie shook her head at such fanciful thinking. What were the odds of not one, but two people in witness protection ending up here? Why did people kill? Money? Revenge? Love? Wrong time, wrong place? Without knowing how the man had died, Addie had little to work with.

"Mademoiselle Foster, are you ill?"

She turned at the heavily accented voice behind her. Chef Henri, dressed in chef whites, stood before her. This was perfect. She didn't know how she'd get a chance to speak with him.

"Chef Henri, how lovely to see you again," she replied. "And I'm fine, thank you. Why would you think I'm ill?"

The older man bowed slightly before her.

"In all the years I have known you, not once have you passed on my macaroni au fromage. When I heard a young woman named Addie ordered a salad, I had to check."

Addie laughed at his joke. At least she hoped it was his attempt at one. Chef Henri was a difficult man to understand.

"I assure you, I'm fine. Bathing suit season is right around the corner. Thought I'd get a jump on eating healthier."

"Ah," he agreed, although his tone said otherwise.

Not knowing where to start, Addie raised a hand, gesturing to the people eating lunch.

"Business seems to be doing well."

He arched one brow, looking every inch the classically trained French chef he was. "And why would it not?"

"Oh…uh…I just meant with another French restaurant opening in Ocean Grove…" She trailed off, knowing it sounded even worse than it did in her head.

"Zut alors! That man? He was no more than a peasant. And certainly not a threat to me." Henri broke off, muttering in French. And even though Addie didn't speak the language, she got the gist of what he was saying.

"I meant no disrespect, Chef," she said by way of apology.

Henri shook his head. "It no longer matters, as the vermin is dead."

The coldness of his tone sent a chill down Addie's spine.

"Now, if you'll excuse me, I have real French cooking to attend to." He stalked away, leaving Addie more unsettled than ever.

Could he have killed Chef Guillaume?

A few moments later, a waiter brought her lunch and bill. She handed him some cash, refused the offer of change, and left the restaurant. All on auto-pilot. So much so, she didn't respond to her name being called.

"Hey! Are you okay? I called your name a half a dozen times."

Addie blinked before spotting Jonah sitting in his unmarked car at the curb in front of her. "What? Oh, sorry. I must have been lost in thought." She dredged up a smile. "How was your morning?"

Did the M.E. come up with a cause of death?

She wanted to know but didn't dare ask. He wouldn't be at liberty to tell her anyway.

"Why don't I give you a ride back to the store?" he countered.

Addie suddenly remembered how creeped out she'd felt coming there and took him up on his offer. She got in, wondering how to mention it to Jonah without his overre-acting. Well, in his defense, he was a cop. And her life was a bit…uh…strange.

She got in, balancing her to-go salad on her knees, and clicked her seatbelt.

"Thank you." Addie blew out a breath, gathering the courage to start the conversation she had no desire to have.

"You might as well tell me," he prompted gently as he pulled away from the curb. "The smile was all fake and never reached your beautiful eyes."

"Remind me never to play poker with you," she quipped, with a lightheartedness she didn't feel.

"You're stalling," he commented as he drove.

"He's back."

Jonah didn't say anything as he made an abrupt turn down a side street. After pulling into the curb, he shut off the motor and turned to her.

"Tell me."

She turned to face him. "On the way to the restaurant, I had a feeling. A bad one. That creepy feeling when you know someone is watching you. And not in a good way." Addie let out a shaky breath she felt like she'd been holding for the past thirty minutes. "It was him. I know it."

"What did you do?"

"I ran into the restaurant. I had to escape the awful feeling." She shuddered.

"Did you notice anyone? Anything out of the ordinary?"

"No. I had my shades on and looked around, trying not to be obvious. Just the normal people in the square."

Jonah pounded his fists against the steering wheel.

"Feel better?" she asked him, sliding one hand up and down the tight muscles of his arm.

"Not really. Maybe if I could do that to his face…"

Addie stifled a laugh. "That's my tough guy. Look, we knew he wouldn't just give up. Stop."

"You're right, of course, but I had hoped," Jonah said on a sigh. He turned the motor back on and glanced at the dash clock. "I'm really sorry, but I have to get back to work. I'll take you to the store."

She wanted to ask him about the autopsy but didn't. "Of course," she said instead.

"I know you know this and don't want to hear it again." He sneaked a quick glance at her. "You have to be careful. No more going alone to get lunch."

Addie twisted her purse strap in her hands but didn't reply. Yes, she knew. No, she didn't want to hear it again. "You're right. I know. But for how long, Jonah? He, or whomever, is the one doing wrong. Not me. Yet, I'm the one who has to pay. Has to change their life." She didn't say she was *the victim* because she refused to see herself that way.

"I know, honey. But what I know even more is that I want a life with you, Addie. I want you on this earth for sixty more years. And if it means being more careful until we get him, then so be it."

He pulled over in front of the store. Turning, Jonah wrapped one ebony curl around his finger before pushing it back behind her ear. "And I know it's easy for me to say and harder for you to do. I know."

And with those couple words, the tension slid from her body, replaced by a warmth she associated with him.

"I know. I want that, too. I promise." She leaned over to kiss him before undoing her seatbelt. "But you have to promise also. I want a life with you, too."

Jonah nodded, his dark eyes filled with emotion.

Addie exited the car while she still could. With every ounce of her being, she wanted to ask him to drive. Anywhere. Just take them away from there. Away from this madness they'd found themselves embroiled in yet again. But this was real life, not a novel or movie.

She turned and waved before heading into the store.

"And where have you been, young lady?" Grey asked the second the shop door closed behind her. His grin from ear to ear took the sting from his words.

She held up the bag, knowing he wouldn't miss the restaurant's emblem on it. *Three, two, one...*

"So, is Henri just an irritable Frenchman?" Grey paused for what she knew was dramatic effect. "Or is he a murderer?"

---

8

*A*ddie stifled a groan. Or maybe a laugh. Grey brought out the worst in her. The last thing she wanted was to encourage his dramatic flair. Even if she had just wondered the same thing. She took a seat behind the counter and opened her salad. After drizzling on the dressing and annoying Grey, she finally answered.

"Well, he's definitely the first. Who knows about the second?"

"Ah ha! So, you think he murdered Chef Guillaume, too. I knew it."

Grey rambled on, apparently not noticing her attempts to rein him in. Or ignoring them, more likely.

"Who killed the chef may be the least of my problems."

"Oh. Oh!" Grey exclaimed. He ran around the counter and dragged one of the stools next to her. "He's back, isn't he?"

Addie took a bite of her salad, even though it now tasted like sawdust and her stomach threatened to revolt. But she needed the protein.

"I had a weird feeling today while walking to get lunch.

You know, where you feel like someone is watching you." She waved a hand behind her head. "And the little hairs all stand on end."

"Oh, Addie," he breathed, running a hand down her arm. "Tell me."

So she did. And then she told him Jonah's reaction.

"Damn straight!" he agreed. "And before you start voicing your objections, don't. I know. You don't want to live your life that way. You don't want to be a victim. Well, I don't want to bury my best friend." Grey slumped on the stool next to her, his eyes suspiciously bright.

And all the fight left her, swirling away as though she was a balloon someone had popped. Her eyes burned.

"I know."

Addie put aside her mostly untouched salad. *No way am I eating that now.* She then bent down and stroked the faces of her lovely dogs. The girls appreciated the sneaked bits of chicken from her salad.

Without looking at him, Addie asked, "How do we end this?"

"I'm glad you asked."

She raised her head and watched Grey pull a well-folded piece of paper from his wallet. The ghost of a smile curled her lips.

"Is that what I think it is?"

Grey shook the paper, smoothing out the wrinkles.

"If you think this is a copy of the possible perp list from months ago, then yes," he replied with a smirk. "Oh, and I may have added a few suspects."

Addie's smile bloomed. Jonah hated it when they used "cop speak," as he called it. Grey loved saying the word "perp." All those TV detective shows had warped his mind. She grabbed the list from his hands and laughed. The list *had* grown.

"Every guy I've ever known is on here." She squinted to try to decipher his deplorable handwriting. "Did you really include your brother?"

"I did indeed. After all, there was that moment when you two...well, you know."

Laughter poured from her. "Harper and I never 'you know.' I had a huge crush on him as a teenager, and he didn't know I existed. Surely, he isn't stalking me now. And from wherever he is in Europe."

Addie took a red pen from the holder on the counter and drew a huge line through his name.

"Well, okay, I guess. He has been photographed recently with that model in Milan. But we have to make sure we don't skip anyone."

Addie tapped a nail on another name. "Mr. Welsh from the bank? Are you kidding? He was old when my mother was still alive. She'd take me in with her, and he'd let me choose whatever flavor lollipop I wanted."

"And maybe he wants to give you more than a lollipop now," Grey suggested, eyebrows waggling.

"Blech! The man is older than dirt. And Mr. Welsh has never said one even remotely inappropriate thing to me. That's just wrong, Grey."

The red pen flew across his name.

"Jonah said we have to put everyone on and then take them off as we eliminate them. So, that's what I did." He grinned. "Well, except for the eliminate part."

"Oh, really? Jonah said this? When?"

Grey's smile slipped. Addie could almost see the wheels turning in his brain. He held up both hands, as if in surrender.

"Uh, maybe a few weeks ago when we grabbed a beer."

"You know I love you guys becoming friends and hanging out. What I do not love is you and he making me the topic of conversation on these outings. You don't get to discuss me in my absence. I'm the one being targeted by…well, someone. That fact alone makes me worthy of being in the conversation. And then there's basic human respect."

Addie stood so she could pace the small space behind the counter. *Men!* She clenched and unclenched her hands. The girls, sensing her distress, tried to pace with her, almost tripping her. She leaned one hip against the counter.

Grey glanced at her, not at all looking chagrined as she'd hoped.

"Boy, is Jonah in trouble." He drew out the last word for several more syllables than it possessed.

"Jonah? Aren't you forgetting someone?"

Grey took a sudden interest in something on his phone. "Can't imagine who," he replied.

"Hey, Addie, is it okay if I leave now? I have finals coming up."

Addie turned to Erin. "Of course. I don't miss that even one little bit."

Erin's smile slid into a frown. "I hear you. Of course, I wasn't thinking about that when I applied to the graduate program at UNCW."

"But you're going after an advanced degree in English Lit. I'm so proud of you!"

Erin grinned. "Thanks, Addie. It means a lot coming from you. And you, too, could get a masters."

Addie laughed, happy to have something else to think about. "I barely have time to breathe these days. And honestly, I am not a fan of being a student again. I love the freedom of reading what I want to read, and not 'required' reading. And don't get me started on exams and papers. No, thanks."

"Way to sell it," Grey sniped. "Besides, our Addie is more

concerned with getting Jonah to marry her and then pushing out babies."

"Remind me again why we're friends?" Addie replied.

"Because you love me, and I keep you on your toes."

"Yeah, sure. Jonah will ask me to marry him when he's ready."

"But what will you say? Inquiring minds want to know," Grey joked.

"That is for me to know and you, and Jonah, to find out." Addie blew a raspberry in his direction before turning back to Erin. "Go before you become further embroiled in his madness."

Erin laughed. "Consider me gone."

A customer approached, and Addie chatted with the woman while she rang up her purchases. She glanced once at Grey, who appeared to be ready to burst. Who knew what was up with him?

When the customer left and no one else stood within fifty feet of them, Grey tapped her on the arm. "So, what's the plan?"

"Plan?" she asked, all innocence and wide eyes.

His striking blue ones narrowed. "Don't make me beg."

Addie laughed. Grey really was a grown up toddler at times. All impatience and inability to delay gratification.

"Honestly, I don't know. Talking with Henri raised more questions than it answered. I love his food, but I don't really know him. He's always so stiff, formal, keeping people at a distance." She closed her eyes for a moment, remembering their conversation. A chill swept over her. She opened her eyes and glanced at Grey. "He seemed like himself until I mentioned the other chef's death. Then a hardness came over his face. His words dripped ice. He actually said, 'I'm glad the vermin is dead.' Can you believe that?"

Grey's eyes bugged. "He said that?"

"Word for word. But his tone and the flatness of his eyes scared me more." Addie shuddered. "I wonder if Jonah will have a chat with him."

"Well, first they have to discover cause of death."

"His autopsy is today. I think Jonah might be there now. He was in a hurry when he dropped me off."

"And then there's motive. Henri has a pretty clear one," Grey suggested.

"Someone's been watching Law and Order again," Addie quipped. "Jonah will be so pleased."

"I may not be a detective, but I could do a better job than Deputy Do Wrong."

Addie giggled. Grey's nickname for Jonah's "partner" never failed to make her laugh.

"True. Still, Jonah hates it when we get involved."

A grimace marred Grey's handsome face. "Well, we did get him shot once. He may have a fair point."

A sharp pain pierced Addie's chest. "Yes, yes, we did," she whispered.

Last summer when her hairdresser had been stabbed to death, with Addie mere feet away in the front of the salon, she and Grey had taken it upon themselves to "solve" her murder. It ended terribly, with Jonah getting shot right in front of them while trying to protect them. And even though he was fine now, Addie had never managed to let go of the guilt. It was her fault, and Grey's, that Jonah almost died that night.

"Oh, honey, I'm so sorry." Grey wrapped her in his arms. "I didn't mean to bring that up."

She leaned into his solid chest for a few moments before sniffing and pulling away.

"No worries. It's not like I don't think of it on my own. But that's my point. We have to be careful. Let Jonah handle this."

"Okaaayyyyy."

"Grey, I mean it." She fixed him with her stop-mud-in-midair stare. Not that it ever worked on him. "No snooping. No digging into things that don't concern us. Got it?"

"Yes, Mom," he quipped.

"Thank you."

Addie didn't think for one moment he meant what he said. She knew him too well. Time would tell. She turned away from him, planning on putting her uneaten salad in her office fridge, when he stopped her with a hand on her arm.

"Just one more question, then."

"Yes?"

"What's the other plan?"

Addie tilted her head, not sure what he was referring to.

"'Other plan?'"

"You know, to catch your stalker."

And just like that, what little she'd eaten threatened to come right back up.

"Oh, that." Addie sat back down and placed her head in her hands.

"It's going to be okay, Addie. Jonah will find him."

"And yet he hasn't. This man, person, flits in and out of my life, leaving terror in his wake. How am I supposed to have a normal life?"

"Well, it's not like you had a very 'normal' life to start." Grey winced. "What I mean is, beyond the crazy, obsessive guy, you still have terrifying prophetic nightmares."

"Gee, thanks."

"You know what I mean."

Addie let out a pent-up breath. "Yes, I know."

"And as terrible as those things are, this is so much worse. This guy, whoever he is, means to hurt you."

"Or worse, hurt Jonah."

"You know I like Jonah, honey, but *you* are my BFF, not him."

"Yes, I know. But he is the love of my life. I do *not* intend to lose him. He and I have plans. Big plans that involve babies and many, many years together." Addie sniffed and widened her eyes in the age old trick women have to prevent crying.

"Babies? There's been talk of babies? Oh my, do the Aunties know? There'll be no stopping them."

"As if we could stop them now." Addie shook her head, near tears replaced by laughter. "Jonah and I talked about babies from the very beginning. Neither of us is getting any younger."

Grey arched one perfect blond brow. "Is there something you haven't told me, Missy?"

"What?" Laughter overtook her. "Oh! No, Grey, there aren't any babies in there yet. And knowing you, you'll know before I do."

"True. Is it time to start tracking your cycle? I can help. They make apps for that."

She knew he wasn't kidding.

"Slow down, Uncle Grey. We aren't there yet."

Grey nodded. "That man needs to put a ring on it first," he joked, quoting his demi-goddess, Beyoncé.

"We already live together. The next logical step is marriage. And Jonah will ask me when he's ready." She wagged a finger at Grey. "And no pressure from the peanut gallery."

Grey nodded. "Got it. I'll keep the Aunties off his back."

"And you."

"Fine. But just remember, those eggs of yours aren't getting any younger!"

9

When the last customer left for the day, Addie collapsed onto one of the comfy couches she had in the store to encourage shoppers to sit and read. She kicked off her sandals and propped her feet on the coffee table. With the return of summer-like weather came the crowds to her small beach town. And though many grumbled about traffic and longer wait times in restaurants, she didn't mind. Because people at the beach liked to read. Which meant they loved to visit Smiling Dog Books.

"Whew! What a day," commented Grey as he plopped down on a couch opposite her. "I thought they'd never leave."

"You mean the paying customers who keep my little bookstore afloat?"

Grey picked a thread off his polo shirt. "Yes, them."

Addie laughed as she stretched her tired neck muscles, swiveling her head back and forth. "Some of us have to work for a living, dear."

"Just saying," he muttered.

A quick rap of knuckles on the front door ended whatever else he might have added.

"Can't they see the closed sign?" Grey groused. He then grinned at Addie. "You're the owner. You go see who's there."

"I'm also the one being stalked. You go with me, tough guy."

She stood, slipped on her shoes, and headed for the door. Grey kept pace with her, as she knew he would. She approached the door, not rushing. They both stopped a few feet away from it. There, on the other side, stood her dapper customer from yesterday.

Was it only yesterday?

Addie flipped the lock and held open the door, motioning for the man to enter.

"Mr. Martin, I didn't expect to see you again so soon. Come in."

"Please, call me Robert. And thank you. I didn't realize you'd be closed already. Please forgive the intrusion."

"No worries, Robert. Is there something I can help you with?"

She fought the urge to step away from the stranger. His piercing blue eyes held hers, and she refused to break his gaze. While he hadn't done anything in the least bit threatening, a chill ran through her.

Could he be my stalker?

Just as quickly, Addie dismissed the notion. She shook her head. This is what the stalker had reduced her to. A ball of paranoia. She bit back a nervous giggle.

"I so enjoyed the book I bought yesterday that I thought I'd stop in and get a few more before I leave town," Robert offered by way of explanation.

"Oh? Leaving so soon?" inquired Grey, not even trying to hide the open curiosity on his face. "I thought you were staying in Ocean Grove for a few days?"

Addie watched Robert peer at Grey before answering.

The older man seemed to be taking stock of her friend. She had no idea why or what it could possibly mean.

"Good memory, Grey. It was my intention to stay, but I've been called back." He smiled at Addie. "A work thing. You understand."

"Of course," murmured Addie, having no clue at all.

"And what line of work did you say you were in, Robert?" Grey asked at the same time.

Addie counted to ten in her head. BFF or not, he could be annoying.

"I don't believe I said," he replied, his tone a bit chilly. But then he glanced at Addie, and his face softened. "I work for the government, based in D.C."

"Well, now that my friend is through grilling you, Robert, why don't you see what other books you'd like?"

"Thank you. I'll only be a moment."

Addie turned and went behind the counter, dragging Grey with her. When Robert headed to the local history section, she glared at him.

"Now you're a spy?" she asked in a heated whisper.

"No, but our new friend may be. 'Works for the government' in D.C.? What else could he be?" he returned, also in a whisper.

"About a thousand different things off the top of my head. Drop it!" She grabbed the two dog leashes, clipping one on each Sheltie. "Do me a favor, Grey, and take the girls out one last time. I want to lock up and leave as soon as our customer is finished."

"You want me to leave you alone with *him*?"

"You'll be right out front, and I'll be fine." She made a shooing gesture with her hands.

"Fine. But don't blame me when he chops you up into tiny bits." He glanced down at the girls, who pranced at their feet, oblivious to the sudden tension. "Let's go, girls."

Addie gritted her teeth before turning to her laptop. She meant to close out her email in preparation to leave, but the words "Yellow might not be your color" in the subject line of an unopened email caught her eye. She clicked to open it. After several seconds, Addie gasped and grabbed for the counter as she felt the blood drain from her face.

"Where did your watchdog run off to?"

She whipped up her head to find Robert standing there, three books in his hands, but no words came. She reached behind her for the stool, leaning one hip against it as she locked her knees to keep from collapsing.

Robert leaned forward, over the counter, as if to grab her, but Addie shrank away from his grasp.

"I didn't mean to frighten you, Miss Foster," he stated. "I mean you no harm."

Before she could formulate a reply, the bells over the door tinkled, announcing Grey's return. She waved one shaking hand to grab her friend's attention. Her chest hurt with the effort to suck in air. She stood there, every muscle in her body seemingly frozen.

"Grey!" she screamed when rational thought finally returned.

The man in question took one look at her face and raced to the desk, two barking dogs in his wake.

"Addie! What happened?" He turned to the customer. "What did you do to her?"

Addie shook her head. Forgetting all about their customer, she pointed to her laptop. "He *was* watching me today. Look!"

Grey gave Robert one more glare before joining her behind the counter. He read the email she pointed to. A soft gasp followed by an imaginative string of curses erupted from him.

Before she could react, Grey pulled out his phone. She

watched him hit a preset number, wait a moment, then bark, "You need to get here. Now."

"May I be of assistance?" Robert asked, his faint British accent more pronounced.

Shaking off the encroaching shock, Addie shook her head.

"I am so terribly sorry, Robert, to have dragged you into this, uh, situation." She gestured to the books he still held in one hand. "Please consider those a gift or an apology. Grey, could you show Robert out, please?"

Addie collapsed onto the stool behind her. Gracey and Lily crowded around her legs, offering canine support. A low whine came from both. She rubbed their silky heads, trying to focus on her breathing. In. Out. Her vision had thankfully lost the dimness around the edges that usually heralded her fainting. Jonah would be here any moment. He would know what to do. And Grey would deal with Robert. As cowardly as it felt, she couldn't handle one more thing right now. Not after reading that email.

Please hurry...

Still shaking, Addie lowered herself to the floor. Both dogs clambered into her lap, and she buried her face in their fluffy coats.

"Where is she?" sounded as the bells over the door jingled.

"Here," Addie whispered into Lily's fur, knowing Jonah couldn't hear her. But he was there. She felt better already.

She kept her eyes closed, focused on her breathing. She heard a mixture of male voices above her but blocked them out while she gathered herself. And then she felt his strong arms around her.

"I'm here, Addie. I've got you," Jonah whispered against her forehead while he kissed her softly.

"It was him," she croaked through her dry throat. "He was watching m-m-me today. Oh, Jonah, I can't keep doing this," she cried before lowering her head and sobbing into his broad chest.

She kept her eyes squeezed tight as he lifted her. She felt him carry her across the store before placing her on the sofa she'd recently vacated. What he said next caught her by surprise.

"And who exactly are you?" Jonah sounded gruff, like when they'd first met.

She glanced up to see Robert approach Jonah, hand extended.

"I'm Robert Martin. And you are…?"

Addie smothered a laugh. Jonah was so used to asking the questions.

"I'm Jonah Wolfe, Addie's boyfriend." He ignored Robert's hand.

"I only meant to purchase these books," Robert held up his other hand, books still clutched, "but something happened, although I'm not quite sure what." He tilted his head toward Addie.

Horrified at dragging this stranger into their drama, Addie stood, closing the space between her and Jonah. She placed a hand on his arm.

"Mr. Martin merely came in to buy more books on local history and had the misfortune of getting caught up in this mess." She summoned a smile for her customer. "Again, my apologies, Mr. Martin. Grey will be happy to show you out, won't you, Grey?"

Grey opened his mouth to reply but never had the chance as Jonah took a step toward the stranger.

"You just happened to be here, after hours, when this happened. Whatever this is." He turned back to her. "Addie, what happened? I get a frantic call from Grey, saying, 'Get here.' So I did." He broke off, breathing hard, all his love, and fear, for her in his eyes.

Addie took him by the hand, leading him behind the counter. She swiped a finger across the mousepad to "wake up" her computer.

"There," she said in a small, shaky voice while pointing at the screen.

Jonah grabbed her hand in his before leaning forward to read the email.

"I saw you today, Adelaide, walking through the square. You knew I was there, didn't you? I watched you look around. But you couldn't see me. Did you enjoy your lunch from Henri's? Or were you too afraid to eat? You should be afraid. Because I'm coming for you. And he cannot save you. No one can."

The email lacked a signature, as the note on her front door had last year. Addie watched Jonah's hands curl into fists. His breath grew labored. He then turned to her, tipping up her face with a finger under her chin.

"No one will hurt you, Addie. I promise. Not this person. Not anyone."

He tucked her into his side. For one brief moment, Addie felt the weight of his presence. Felt safe. Just for a moment.

"Now *you* have some explaining to do, Mr. Martin."

Addie watched something, some fleeting emotion, flash across the stranger's face. Then the polite but aloof mask fell back into place. He placed the books on the counter and raised both hands, spreading them wide, as if in entreaty.

"My name is Robert Martin. I am here for a few days on vacation from D.C., where I have lived since childhood. I do not know what is happening here. I am not a part of it. I came in to buy some books. That is why one comes to a bookstore."

Addie held her breath as a muscle ticked in Jonah's jaw.

"Normally, Mr. Martin, I would agree with you. But then these are far from normal circumstances. Did Addie happen to mention I'm a detective here in Ocean Grove?"

He added a smile, the one that showed a lot of teeth and reminded Addie of his last name.

Robert didn't appear in the least impressed, nor intimidated, by this information. Rather, he drew himself up to his full height and leaned in almost imperceptibly.

"While I admire a man who has chosen to dedicate his life to public service, I'm not sure what it has to do with me." He drew out his wallet and placed a fifty-dollar bill on the counter, then turned to Addie. "Miss Foster, I am sorry for whatever trouble you may be having. I will see myself out."

And that's exactly what he did, while the three of them watched him go. Grey roused himself and followed Robert, locking the door behind him. Addie waited for his usual snarky remark, but none came.

Jonah ran a hand up her arm. "I know this scares you. It scares me, too. Which is why you *will* be more careful and not go anywhere alone. Understood?"

She nodded, afraid to speak lest the tears she fought to hold in broke loose.

"And Grey, I need you to understand the importance of this as well. I know we've all loosened up a bit after not hearing from him since before Thanksgiving. That ends now. No more taking chances. No more going out alone." He dragged a hand through his dark hair. "I can't be with her every minute of every day, so I need to depend on you, Grey. Got it?"

A subdued Grey nodded. "I would die for her. She knows that."

Jonah nodded.

The tears Addie was fighting to hold back won, coursing down her face. "No one is dying, especially not *for* me. I'll be careful. I won't go anywhere alone. I won't take any chances. But the same goes for you guys. No one knows what this maniac is capable of." She ended on a sob, burying her face in her hands.

Addie felt Jonah gather her in his arms. Her tears soaked his dress shirt. She didn't care. Just feeling him next to her, hearing his heartbeat beneath her ear was enough for now. Jonah was safe.

But for how long?

10

*G*etting ready for bed that night, Addie took some melatonin to help her sleep. She crossed her fingers, hoping the medication would also offer a dreamless sleep. The stress of the day left her shaky and unsettled, as if last night hadn't already taken its toll. After a mostly silent dinner, she and Jonah had tried to watch a Netflix movie, but she doubted she could say the title of it.

She tumbled into her side of the bed. Jonah, reading something on his phone, plugged it into the charger on the nightstand. He turned back to her, staring, as if trying to assess her stress level.

Addie smiled at him, knowing how much he hated seeing her cry. And she'd already subjected him to enough today.

"You haven't asked about the autopsy." He placed the back of his hand against her forehead. "Hmm…feels cool," he joked.

"I've learned to mind my own business," she muttered in answer to his unasked question.

One dark brow, the one she loved with the scar bisecting it, raised, but he remained silent.

"I have," she protested. The stern voice she hoped for dissolved into giggles. "Okay, fine. Of course I want to know what killed Chef. But I've learned not to ask things you aren't free to answer."

Jonah kissed her forehead. "Yes, you have. And thank you for not making this whole thing any more awkward."

He clicked off his lamp and slid down into the bed. Addie did the same, ducking under his raised arm and laying her head on his chest.

"It's not for a lack of curiosity. In case you wondered."

"Oh, no need to wonder," he said with a smile and kiss. "It'll be public record soon enough."

She snuggled deeper into him, her eyelids growing heavy. "I need to sleep. You know the heavy sleep where you don't dream, don't even move all night." She covered a yawn.

"I've got you, Addie. Go to sleep," Jonah murmured against the top of her head.

"ADDIE, GRAB MY HAND. I CAN HELP YOU."

The man's voice sounded so far away. She clung to Jonah, refusing to leave his side.

"I'm going to get you out of here, Jonah. Help will come. I promise." She picked up his hand and held it to her mouth. He didn't move; just lay there so still. Too still.

A loud bang in the other room drew her attention. Someone was back there, in the kitchen. But who? And what were they doing?

"Please, Addie, let me help you. It isn't safe."

The man pleaded to her, but she turned a deaf ear. She wouldn't leave Jonah.

"We don't have much time. Jonah can't help you, but I can. Please."

Tears coursed down her face, dripping onto Jonah's slack one.

The other voice sounded vaguely familiar, but it didn't matter. She couldn't, wouldn't leave Jonah.

She turned to face the shadowy figure of a man just outside of the light from her phone. His hands reached for her, beckoning her.

"I will not leave him. I've already called 9-1-1. Help is coming."

The creak of a door swinging open caught her attention. Addie huddled over Jonah in a last-ditch effort to protect him. But from what?

"No, I won't leave him!" Addie screamed. The sound of her cries woke her. Lurching up in bed, she turned to Jonah's side, only to find it empty.

"Jonah!" she yelled, breaking the otherwise quiet of her bedroom.

And then, almost as if in a dream, he appeared in the bathroom doorway, towel knotted around his hips. His dark hair wet, dripping water down his face and chest.

"What's wrong, Addie?" he asked as he approached the bed. "I'm right here."

The sight of him, alive and obviously unharmed, was all it took to send her into a wave of tears. Addie leaped out of bed and threw her arms around him.

"You're okay," she breathed into his damp chest.

He closed his arms around her.

"Hey, it's okay. I'm fine. You're fine." He tightened his grip on her. "Bad dream, I guess."

She nodded against his chest, taking a moment to pull herself together. And then it hit her like a rogue ocean wave. She pulled from his arms to stare into his face.

"Oh my goodness. That's why he seemed so familiar to me. I knew I'd heard his voice before."

"Who's voice, Addie?"

"Robert Martin's voice. He's the one who pulled me from the fire last summer. The voice I'd heard in my dream before it happened."

After dropping that bomb on Jonah – and herself, really – Addie threw on shorts and a T-shirt to let the girls out. She sent them into her fenced back yard, then busied herself in the kitchen, making breakfast. Although she was a terrible cook, she could handle breakfast, and she needed something to do. Anything to keep her hands busy. And her mind.

Jonah entered the kitchen, dressed for work. He'd already rolled back the sleeves of his dress shirt. "Any more revelations?" he joked.

"Nope. Just scrambling some eggs. Mind seeing to the toast?"

"Of course not."

He stood next to her, placing four slices in the toaster. Jonah bumped her with his hip.

"So, Martin isn't a stranger after all."

"Not sure I would go that far," she replied.

Addie flipped off the burner and divided the eggs onto two plates. She then poured coffee and juice before sitting at the table. After a minute, Jonah brought a plate with the rye toast.

After they'd started eating, Jonah looked up at her. "Tell me."

Addie nodded and swallowed the food in her mouth.

"When Robert Martin first came in the other day, he seemed so familiar to me. But I didn't know why. I knew I'd never seen him before. And yet..."

"You couldn't put your finger on it?" Jonah suggested.

"Exactly. It always annoys me when something is right there, just out of reach, in your memory. I knew I'd never *seen* him before."

Jonah took a bite of his toast, seemingly also digesting what she'd said.

"Tell me about your latest dream."

"It was like last year when I dreamed about him. He was in the dream, but I couldn't quite see him. His face – most of him, really – was in shadow." She let out a breath and closed her eyes. "He wanted to save me. Kept calling my name, reaching for me, begging, really. But I wouldn't listen. I couldn't l-l-l-eave y-y-you." Addie swiped at the tears running down her face.

"Promise me, Addie, that you won't sacrifice your own life for mine. Ever."

Pain flooded her chest. "How can I make that promise, Jonah? Please don't ask it of me."

"How would I live with myself, Addie, if you died trying to save me?" He closed his eyes as though the very thought were too much to bear.

"So then you know, understand, how I feel. Jonah let's promise each other to see this thing through. Figure it out without either of us having to ask that of the other."

Jonah's brow furrowed, then he nodded. "Tell me everything you know about him. Everything he said. Don't leave anything out."

She told him what little she knew. Jonah sat, listening to her without interruption.

"Saying he works 'for the government' could mean anything. Especially in D.C." Jonah ran a hand through his hair, breakfast abandoned.

"Grey and I thought the same thing. But what could it mean? And why wouldn't he just come out and say what he does? The whole thing makes him sound like a spy or something," Addie said before laughing at the thought. "Can you imagine? A spy? Right here in Ocean Grove? A spy who knows me by name?"

But Jonah didn't laugh with her.

"That's what worries me, Addie. He knew you by name. Came looking for you," he grunted.

She felt her jaw drop and couldn't do a thing about it. "You almost sounded serious for a moment, Jonah. It's a ridiculous notion." Addie laid down her fork, noticing her hand trembling. Couldn't do anything about that either. "What are you suggesting, Jonah? Why would a spy, for lack of a better word, know me by name and seek me out? Me? I own an indie bookstore in a small beach town. Doesn't exactly scream intrigue."

The words had exploded from her in one breath. She sat back in her chair, breakfast forgotten, staring at Jonah, willing him to make this better. To tell her this was ridiculous.

"Maybe for the same reason three thugs from Interpol's most wanted list came here last summer. Looking for you, Addie. We never did get an answer on why Viktor Juric and his henchmen tried to kill you."

An old, familiar dread in the form of icy sweat trickling down her spine reared its ugly head.

Could he be right?

"Surely, you don't think…" Addie didn't even know how to finish the sentence. Nothing made any sense. But neither did having them after her, not to mention trying to kill her, last year.

Jonah got up and crossed to the dogs' bowls, scraping bits of egg into each. "I don't know, Addie. I honestly don't know what to think." He turned to face her. "What I do know is that with everything going on, you need to be more careful than ever."

Addie watched him take out his phone to make a call. She wondered who he needed to speak to at this early hour. She didn't have to wait long.

"Morning, Grey. Yes, I know it's early. Tough. I have to leave for work in less than fifteen minutes. That's how long you have to get here. Thanks."

He ended the call and slid his phone back in his pocket. "Today, and for the foreseeable future, you will *not* go anywhere alone. Got it?" He stopped talking until she nodded. "Good. I'm heading to work as soon as Grey rolls out of bed and gets here. First thing I'm going to do is find out anything I can on Robert Martin. If that's even his name."

Jonah walked to the table, leaning down to kiss her. "Thank you for breakfast. Need to get ready."

Giving up on eating anything else, Addie got up and cleaned the kitchen. Before she knew it, Grey stood outside her kitchen sliding door, hand raised to knock. That man never came in the normal way.

The girls, seeing their beloved "Uncle Grey," rushed the door, barking and twirling in tight circles. Addie crossed the kitchen and unlocked the door for him.

"That was quick," she joked, taking in his slightly mussed hair. "Did you just get out of bed?"

Grey nodded. "About ten seconds after Jonah's phone call."

Addie winced. "Sorry."

"No worries." He held up an overnight bag. "But I'll need to shower here before we head into the shop."

"Of course. Jonah will be out in a moment. Then it's all yours."

Jonah walked into the kitchen and raised a hand in greeting to Grey. "Thanks, man. I have to go." He leaned down, kissing Addie once more. "Call or text me with anything. If you even so much as have a bad feeling about anything, call me." He stooped to pet the girls before leaving, taking a bit of her heart with him.

Addie sighed, watching him leave.

"Ah, young love," Grey quipped.

"I'm going to marry that man. And I may not wait for him to ask me." She let out a shuddering breath. "Life is short, Grey, with no guarantees."

"Amen, sister. Let me grab a shower so we can head to work."

"Great. I have a lot to tell you."

"Already? It's only a little after eight in the morning. What could possibly have happened already?"

"You have no idea."

11

"Shut the front door!" Grey exclaimed an hour later in her car.

Addie laughed at his reaction to her dream, as well as the revelation that Robert Martin starred in it. She kept her eyes on the road, resisting the urge to see the look of shock on his very expressive face.

"Wait a minute...does that mean what I think it means?"

Grey's voice reached a pitch that made Addie want to cover her ears.

"Yes, Robert Martin, or whatever his name is, pulled me from the burning warehouse last year." She stopped at a red light down the block from her store and darted a glance his way. His blond brows met his hairline. "At least that's what Jonah and I believe."

"Oh. My. Goodness. Why?"

She couldn't help laughing at the note in his voice. It landed midway between disbelief and incredulity.

"Uh, thanks? Who knows?" she answered, tongue in cheek.

"Obviously, I'm happy he rescued you." Grey shuddered,

as though remembering just how close she'd come to dying that day. "But I mean how? How did he know? Why did he know? What is he to you?"

And there is the best question of all.

"I don't know the answer to any of those questions, although I wish I did." Addie sighed as she pulled into her parking space behind the bookstore. She turned to Grey. "I know I've never met him before last summer. And that can't even be considered 'meeting him.' I was mostly unconscious."

She got out and opened the hatch for the girls. Excited yips and pink tongues met her.

"What does Jonah think about this?" Grey asked as he grabbed her computer bag.

"Jonah doesn't know what to think either. He's planning to research the man at work. Dig up what he can. Of course, he also has the dead chef to deal with." A hand flew over her mouth. "I didn't mean to sound so…"

"Callous? Unfeeling? Cruel?" suggested Grey.

She swatted him with the end of Lily's leash. "You know what I meant. I found the man insufferable but obviously didn't wish him dead."

"What about the fact that Jonah was there when he 'kicked the bucket,' so to speak?"

"Oh. He didn't say, and I didn't ask. But that is a good question. I hope that doesn't mean Dan is in charge. That man couldn't find his way out of a paper bag, let alone solve a murder."

"Good one, Addie. Sadly, you may be right about that. I don't like him. Not one bit."

"Well, that makes two of us. He's creepy. And lazy. Not sure how he ever made detective."

Addie opened the back door to the bookstore and turned off the alarm. She walked through to the front and let the girls off their leashes behind the counter. After giving each a doggie biscuit, this week's design was a flip-flop from Gertie's bakery, she took out her computer and turned it on.

"What are the odds that Robert Martin is his real name?" she asked Grey.

"Doubt it. Have you Googled him yet?"

"Ah, great minds! That's my first order of business today. But for now, I have to wiz through the shop to tidy up, since we left so abruptly yesterday."

Normally, Addie straightened up after closing to get the store ready for the next day. But last night, she'd been too rattled by the threatening email to do anything.

"I could do it for you," Grey offered.

Addie smiled but shook her head. "Now, I know how much you love me, since you're allergic to cleaning. And I thank you. But this will settle me. Shouldn't take long."

"Well, if you think it's safe, I'll pop next door for coffees for us. I'll lock the door."

"I know I need to be careful, but the store will be locked, and you'll be less than five minutes."

"Do you want your usual?"

Addie grinned at that. He really knew her better than most people in the world. But she still liked to tease him.

"And what would my usual be?"

Grey rolled his eyes. "As if I don't know you. Your coffee preference changes with the season. Since spring doesn't exist here in North Carolina, and it's already ungodly hot in early May, I'll go with a cold beverage. You like it sugary but with a kick of caffeine to start your day. I'd guess an iced Caramel Macchiato. Was I close?"

"Of course you were, as that is exactly my choice." She wrinkled her nose at him. "Am I really that predictable?"

"When it comes to coffee, yes, ma'am. If this were late September into the fall, I'd go with pumpkin spiced anything. December brings peppermint flavored coffee."

Addie held up a hand. "All right already. You win. I really have to spice things up a bit."

"Oh, Addie, I think your life is already as spicy as you can handle. And I'm not talking coffee." He kissed her cheek. "Be right back in two shakes of a lamb's tail."

Addie watched him go, listening for the sound of the lock clicking behind him. Then she got to work. She roamed around the store for a minute, picking up discarded books to reshelve. She hummed an old Garth tune about wild horses as she worked.

But after a moment, she stopped. And listened. Had she heard something? When she didn't hear it again, Addie resumed her straightening and chided herself for her paranoid thoughts. This wasn't the way she wanted to live. Yes, being careful would be prudent. Jumping at every little noise, real or imaginary, would drive her crazy.

Still, she avoided the front of the shop, with its large picture windows, and counted the seconds until Grey's return. At least the girls seemed calm. They may only weigh under twenty pounds each, but they made an excellent early warning system. No one could get in without them both freaking out.

There hadn't been many wayward books to return, so Addie grabbed a dust rag from her office and ran it along the shelves. Although she'd hired a cleaning crew to do the heavy lifting, Addie like to know Smiling Dog Books always looked its best.

She jumped at a series of barks from behind the counter. Addie's heart raced. She gripped the dust cloth.

Please be Grey returning. After all, he only went next door to The Daily Grind for their coffee.

She walked toward the door to the back room, still clutching the dust rag in her hands. She heard what sounded like a key in the lock and held her breath.

Surely, my stalker doesn't have a key.

After a moment, she heard the door open, then close, the lock engaging once again. She let out a ragged breath as Grey materialized in front of her.

"What were you going to do? Strangle me with that thing?" he asked. "I come bearing peace. And coffee," he joked.

The tension in her shoulders melted away. "For all you know, I might know a way to kill a man with this."

One blond brow arched. "Do you?"

Heat creeped along her face. "Well, no, of course not. But a stranger wouldn't know that."

Grey handed her the iced drink. "Here, you may need this more than I knew." He took a sip of his own coffee as he looked around. "Are we ready to open?"

"As ready as I'm going to be."

Addie walked to the front door, flipping the sign, and unlocking it. She walked behind the counter to sit on the stool.

"Here's the thing. I can't stop living my life, Grey. I won't."

"And yet you also want to have a life. With Jonah and the cutie pie babies."

Addie sighed. "Yes, you're right again. So tell me, oh wise one, how do I balance this? How do I get to keep my sanity and my actual life?"

Grey tapped one perfectly manicured finger against his chin. The fact that he got manicures on a regular basis horrified Jonah.

"First, I am so not old. But back to the subject at hand. We figure out who the stalker is, putting it to bed once and for all. Then we make sure the chef murder thing was a one-off, so to speak."

Addie laughed, but the sound didn't give her any comfort.

"Ah, what have we been trying to do for months, Grey?"

He shook his head. "Not so much. You have to admit, we've slacked off a bit."

She wanted to scream, but he was right. As usual.

"Okay, maybe a bit."

Grey held his thumb and pointer finger close together, then spread them as wide as he could. "More than a bit. And who could blame you? Not hearing from the jackass has been a lovely reprieve."

"But it's over now," Addie lamented.

"Yes, it is. And it needs to end for good. Do you really want to live with this hanging over your head?"

"No, Grey, I don't. I want it to end more than you'll ever know. Because this person, whoever he or she is, has put my life on hold. I want things, Grey."

"Yeah, you do!"

"I want to marry Jonah."

"Of course."

"And I want babies before I'm forty."

"Right again."

"But I can't do either of those things with this danger lurking." Her shoulders dropped. "I could never endanger anyone else with this."

The bells over the front door tinkled, signaling their first customer of the morning, and ending their discussion.

Addie saw Grey tap something into his phone as she approached the customer who came in. She hoped it wasn't something she'd regret. Like a text to her aunties, telling them to resume knitting baby booties.

"Good morning, and welcome to Smiling Dog Books. May I help you find anything?"

The woman pulled a piece of paper from her purse. "Oh, yes, please. My sixteen-year-old son has to read a book, uh, *Sold*, by Patricia McCormick. Of course, he has to read it by tomorrow. Guess when he told me?"

Addie stifled a laugh. This was a familiar quandary.

"I'm guessing either late last night or early this morning. Maybe on his way out the door?"

"And you would be right. So, if you tell me you have this, I'll be your new best friend."

Addie laughed aloud this time, liking this woman already.

"Well then, bestie, let me show you where it is."

"Hey, I heard that," came an indignant cry from Grey.

The other woman startled before laughing herself.

"That is my actual best friend, Grey. Ignore him. He's off his meds." She led the way to the teenage fiction section.

"Here's a tip for the future," Addie said. "The local schools all give me their reading lists at the beginning of each school year so I can have the books in stock. Whenever you need one, just give me a call. I'll be happy to place it on hold for you."

"Oh, wow! I'd hug you if it weren't a bit weird," the woman said. "But seriously, thank you. You're a lifesaver."

Addie grabbed a copy of *Sold* off a shelf and handed it to her. "How about something for Mom? Maybe a little something to take your mind off the fact that you have teenagers?"

"Now I *know* you're my new best friend. If you had a margarita on hand, I might leave my husband for you."

She and Addie laughed at her joke.

"Sorry, can't help you there. But I do run a book club here the first Wednesday of each month. And there may be wine involved as well." She handed the woman a brightly colored flyer announcing the club and the list of books to be read for the rest of the year.

"I'm Jane, by the way, and thank you." She glanced at the flyer. "Oh, I've read a few of these. How wonderful! Now, if you could point me to the romance section, the steamier, the better, I'll pick out a present for myself."

"Well, I'm Addie, and let me show you." She walked Jane

to the right section. "I'll be up front when you're ready to check out."

As she walked to the counter, Addie's heart lifted a bit. Yes, life was out of control once again. Yes, a mad stalker was back, threatening her. Yes, the awful nightmares had returned. But she loved this place she'd built, and Jane was exactly who Addie had in mind when she did. Helping people and introducing them to new books made her day.

For now, it would be enough to focus on the positive. She'd deal with the rest. And the feeling of well-being floated along with her as she stepped behind the counter. Lily and Gracey, as if sensing it, stood and stretched before coming to greet her with wagging tails.

"Yes, girls, Mommy is feeling better. We'll figure out this mess."

And we will. Because I have a life to get back to.

The bells over the door danced once again, and Addie turned to greet the newcomer. Her newly minted smile quickly slid from her face, though, when she saw who'd entered.

"Good morning, Miss Foster," greeted Robert Martin. "Forgive me for the interruption. I just stopped by on my way out of town to see how you were after the nasty shock you received yesterday."

Addie opened her mouth to answer, but no words came out. All she could hear was the rush of her own heartbeat.

"What are you doing here?" Grey asked, his voice containing a distinct edge.

Addie shook herself out of the fog that had enclosed her.

"What Grey meant to say was, good morning to you as well, Mr. Martin. I'm fine, thank you. And you?"

She held so still, the muscles in her back felt as though they might snap at any moment. But Addie refused to show any emotion. He might be what he said he was. He might not. He might even be her stalker.

"I'm very well, thank you for asking." He glanced at Grey, his expression giving nothing away. "As I said, I merely stopped in to make sure you had recovered from your nasty shock. I'm on my way home this morning and thought I would check before leaving Ocean Grove."

"You have to admit, your timing is a bit...well, suspect," added Grey.

"If I had any idea what you were talking about, Grey, I might."

"Gentlemen, please lower your voices." Addie looked over

Robert's shoulder to smile at Jane. "Did you find something for yourself?"

Jane, seemingly oblivious to the thick tension in the air, returned the smile. She held up some books. "Something steamy for now, and June's book club novel as well."

"Wonderful!" Addie rang up Jane's purchases, all the while keeping an eye on Grey and Mr. Martin. Goodness only knew what her friend was capable of. "Here you go," she told Jane after completing the sale and placing the books in one of the store's reusable bags.

"Oh, I love these," Jane exclaimed. "And look, you even have 'smiling dogs' on it." She pointed to the picture of the girls on the front of the bag.

"She even has them with her," joked Grey, pointing behind the counter.

"What?" Jane leaned over the countertop. "Oh, my. You're just cute as buttons, aren't you?"

"Would you like to meet them?" Addie asked, aware of Mr. Martin standing there, silently, yet taking in the conversation.

"Oh, could I?"

"Sure. Give me a second." She put a leash on each dog and led them around the counter. Both wagged their tails and stretched their necks to reach Jane's outstretched hands.

"They come to work with me daily and love to greet customers. Gracey, say hello," she commanded her dog. Gracey barked once and held up a paw.

"Oh, my goodness," Jane squealed. She squatted down to pet Gracey's head. "That's adorable."

Lily, as though not happy about being left out, woofed softly next to Addie.

Addie laughed. "Don't worry, Lily, I didn't forget about you. Say hello."

Lily woofed again and raised her paw like her sister had. Jane rewarded her with a pat on the head.

"We have an eight-year-old daughter as well. If she saw these cuties, there'd be no hearing the end of it. That one's dog and horse crazy, for sure."

"Weren't we all at that age?" joked Addie. She liked meeting new customers. Many had become friends, especially those who joined her book club. But right now, with Robert Martin standing a mere ten feet away and never taking his gaze from her, she needed Jane to leave.

Jane gave the girls one final rub each. "Thanks again, Addie. You're a lifesaver. And I'll see you next month, if not sooner."

"I look forward to it," she called to the woman's retreating back.

Addie waited until the door had closed behind Jane to return her attention to her other visitor. "As you can see, I'm fine. Business as usual. Now, is there anything I can help you with?"

"Anything at all," Grey snarked.

She glared at her friend but didn't say anything. No use encouraging him.

Robert Martin stared at her for so long, she had to fight the urge to squirm. It felt as though he memorized every inch of her face. Finally, he dropped her gaze.

"No, Miss Foster. As I said, I only wished to ensure you had recovered from yesterday."

He leaned in the tiniest fraction and looked as though he wanted to say more. But he didn't.

"Very well. Have a safe journey back to D.C.," she wished him.

Robert's head tilted the slightest bit as he once again appeared to struggle with something. The look then disappeared from his face, replaced with a very polite smile.

"Thank you, I will."

Addie and Grey watched him leave without saying another word. When they were once again alone in the store, she turned to him.

"Well, that was, uh, interesting."

Addie couldn't shake the feeling that Robert had been taking stock of her somehow. The penetrating glance of his was not one of a casual acquaintance.

"Wonder what Lover Boy will say about this?" Grey murmured.

Addie groaned. "Let me guess, you already texted him."

"Of course. That's what 'guard dogs' do, isn't it?" Grey smiled at his own joke.

Last summer, when they first met Jonah, after Addie stumbled, literally, over her first dead body, the detective had referred to Grey as her "guard dog." Grey, being perverse as he was, found it all very amusing.

"I'm sure he's busy today. Not sure if the chief will let him investigate the death since he was there and all."

Addie took the girls back behind the counter. She sat in front of her laptop. "Let's see what I can find on our Robert Martin."

———

SEVERAL HOURS LATER, WHILE EATING THEIR LUNCHES, ADDIE groaned.

"Who knew 'Robert Martin' would be such a common name? How will I ever find out anything about him?"

Grey finished chewing a bite of his meatball sub, narrowly missing dripping red sauce on his shirt. "Well, it is a rather bland name that doesn't exactly stick out. I don't suppose you found anything on social media?"

Addie rolled her eyes. "Did he strike you as someone with

a profile? Can't you just see his posted pictures of his dinner or garden?"

"Better yet, maybe a picture of Fifi, his prize-winning Poodle," Grey joked.

"I did try. There were thousands of hits with that name. I'm not sure what else to do now," Addie sighed.

"Gee, if only we knew someone who could investigate this. Maybe someone with, I don't know, a police background."

Addie threw her napkin at Grey. "Funny. He's already on it."

"Good. We may have a potential name for our stalker list," suggested Grey.

Addie shook her head. "I didn't get that vibe."

Grey laughed, almost spitting sweet tea on her. "Do stalkers have a vibe, Addie? And if so, what is it?"

"Go ahead and make fun of me, but I didn't feel uncomfortable around him. Well, that's not entirely true, but he didn't give me the willies. Let's say he didn't creep me out like Dan does."

Grey shuddered. "That man is a walking creepy feeling. I don't know how Jonah tolerates him."

"Maybe because he doesn't have a choice."

The bell over the door rang, breaking her concentration. Addie looked up and stifled a groan. She schooled her features into what she hoped passed for casual disinterest.

"Good afternoon, Addie," the man himself said, as though they'd conjured him.

"Detective Blackwell. To what do we owe this pleasure?" Addie mentally winced at her poor word choice. Nothing about Dan Blackwell gave her any pleasure.

"Detective," Grey muttered. It sounded as though he'd used the full moniker he'd christened him with but coughed over the other words. "We were just now talking about you. You must be psychic."

"Mr. Waverly," Dan returned with a snarl. "Don't you have a job other than hanging out here all day?"

Addie placed one hand on Grey's arm to prevent him from spewing.

"Detective Blackwell, Grey is keeping me company in light of what's happening," she offered by way of explanation. Not that he deserved one.

"Speaking of 'psychics,' didn't you foresee this little event, Addie?" His smile was most likely meant to charm but merely sent chilly shivers through her. "After all, you're the one with the weirdo, prophetic dreams."

The word "prophetic" hit her straight in the heart, not that he could know. Jonah never would have revealed the terrifying dream to this man. She slid off the stool, drawing herself up to her full height. Not that it did much good.

"Was there something I could help you with, Detective Blackwell?"

"Now, Addie, no need to get your feathers ruffled. Since I'm not questioning you at the moment, you can call me 'Dan.'"

I'll give you ruffled feathers!

At her feet, both dogs growled low in their throats. And who said dogs weren't excellent judges of character?

"How may I help you, *Detective*?" Addie repeated. She stared him down, not flinching. Not giving him the satisfaction. With a little glee, she noticed his face harden at her choice of words.

"Well, Addie, it's more about how you can help yourself. And Jonah, of course."

The smirk on his face made Addie clench her hands into fists. But his words left her chilled.

"Wh-wh-what are you talking about?" she stammered.

She felt Grey stiffen next to her, but for once, he remained silent.

"Your boyfriend is with the chief as we speak, going over the events of the other night."

"Why? Jonah already gave his statement, as did I. What else is there to say?"

She willed her pounding heart to slow as her lunch threatened to come back up.

"Who knows? Maybe things aren't as clear as you'd like to think. Maybe being the last person to see a murder victim alive doesn't look good for a detective. Maybe all of your shenanigans reflect poorly on the oh-so-sainted Jonah Wolfe."

Dan tipped his hand, and his obvious dislike and jealousy of Jonah poured out.

"I already told you everything I know, Detective. Several times. So unless you're here to arrest me or buy a book, I'm going to have to ask you to leave."

His beady eyes glared at her, staring what felt like a hole right through her. She saw him wrestle with what he probably wanted to say to her, but he never got the chance. Grey slid out from behind the counter, coming to a stop next to the shorter man.

"I'll be happy to see you out, Detective," he said by way of warning.

"This isn't over, Addie. Not by a long shot. You'd do well to remember that."

With that threat, Dan left the store and her shaking.

"Now, now, Addie, don't let him shake you. He's obviously compensating for a small mind, and a smaller you-know-what."

A brittle laugh erupted from her. "Good one, Grey." She chewed on her lower lip. "But what if he's right? What if Jonah does get into trouble? At the very least, this can't look good for him."

"Why don't we see what happened, if anything, before we go borrowing trouble? Jonah is a straight shooter. He'll tell you if something's up." He walked back behind the counter and wrapped her in his arms for a hug.

"Hey, that's my woman you have there," came an amused male voice from across the room.

"Jonah!"

Addie rushed into his outstretched arms. She wrapped her arms around his waist and clung to him. Pressing her face into his chest, she sniffed and willed away the tears.

"Hey, what's wrong?" Jonah leaned back enough to peer into her face. "Are you crying?"

Addie sniffed. "Of course not. I'm just so glad to see you."

"Tell him about our visitor, Addie," Grey commanded.

"What visitor?" asked Jonah.

At the same time, Addie muttered, "Which one?"

Jonah's dark brow lifted. "Wait. What?"

Addie sighed. "Grey, I love you, but you're a pain in the you-know-what."

"True, and never claimed to not be," he joked.

"He is both brutally honest and exceedingly self-aware," Addie agreed.

"Someone start talking," Jonah commanded.

They both did, at the same time and in a jumbled rush. Addie broke off laughing.

"Grey, can you watch the store for a moment while Jonah and I talk in the office?" She glanced around at a few customers milling about. "This probably isn't the best place."

"Oh, sure, make me miss all the fun," Grey lamented.

Jonah grinned at Grey. "I'll throw you a bone. Chef Guillaume was poisoned, and your friend, Chef Henri, is a person of interest in the murder."

"*W*hat?"

Addie stared at Jonah, trying to comprehend the bomb he'd just dropped. Actually, both of the bombs he dropped.

"I knew it," crowed Grey. "I had a bad feeling Henri was behind this." His blue eyes danced. "It was the salmon mousse! Or in this case, the chocolate mousse."

Jonah stared at Grey, eyes wide as though he contemplated having the other man committed.

"Grey, not everyone has seen Monty Python's, *The Meaning of Life.*" Addie gave Jonah a wan smile by way of apology for her crazy friend. "And anyway, remember the whole innocent until proven guilty thing?" She rubbed her temples with the heel of her hands while her mind whirled.

Could Henri really have killed the other chef?

"No," she cried. "I don't believe that for a minute."

"You know he was less than happy when Guillaume came to town and opened another French restaurant," Grey said. "Maybe Henri killed him out of professional jealousy."

"Hold on, everyone," Jonah said.

"Oooh, maybe he killed him over a woman," Grey added. "You know, a crime of passion."

Jonah held up a hand. "Grey, stop right there. Not one more word," he advised. He turned to Addie. "Are you okay? Do you have a headache?"

"I do. There's too much to think about at one time. First worrying about you, and now Henri. I know he couldn't have done this." She mentally crossed her fingers, hoping she was right.

"Wait. What? Why were you worrying about me?" Jonah asked.

"Oh, Detective Do Wrong thinks you're going down for the murder," Grey said.

Addie closed her eyes and put her head in her hands. "I can't do this right now." She opened her eyes again. "Grey, you mind the store. Jonah, you come with me." She grabbed Jonah's hand, not giving anyone time to argue.

"Is she this bossy in the bedroom?" Grey quipped, earning himself a glare from Jonah.

Addie ignored Grey, knowing from years of experience that was the best course. She tugged Jonah's hand harder and headed for the back of the store. She waited until they were seated in her tiny office with the door closed before saying another word, and then only after swallowing a couple pain relievers from the bottle in her drawer.

"Now that we can have a normal conversation, who starts?" she asked Jonah.

"How about we start with your not one, but two visitors?" he replied.

Addie sighed, knowing she wasn't going to get out of that conversation.

"Well, in order of appearance, first came Robert Martin,

followed very closely by Dan. Which would you care to hear about first?" She wrinkled her nose, letting Jonah know how she felt about the latter.

Jonah leaned back in his chair and loosened his tie. "Wow! Not what I expected to hear. Let's take order of importance and start with the mysterious Robert Martin. What did he want?"

Addie tried not to smile at the gruffness of his voice. It might hurt her head too much. But a protective Jonah was adorable.

"He said he was on his way back to D.C. and wanted to make sure I was 'fine' after yesterday's debacle," she explained.

Jonah stared at her. "And yet your voice says you don't believe him."

"I don't know, Jonah. I don't know what to believe." She twisted a curl around her finger, searching for the right words to convey what she'd felt.

"You're doing the hair thing. Spit it out."

"You know me so well. He seemed very intense, like he was memorizing my face while he spoke. I don't know how to explain it otherwise. But the thing is, I never felt alarmed or creeped out despite it."

"You seemed convinced this morning that Robert Martin is the same man from your dreams. The man who saved your life last summer. Could that be the reason? I can't have it clouding your judgment, even if he is that man."

Addie gaped at him before reining in her temper. "Let's start with I know Robert Martin saved my life last summer. And at the risk of his own. I don't know him, so I can't imagine why he would do that or how he even knew to be there at the moment of the fire."

"Exactly, Addie. How did he know? Is he connected to those Eastern European thugs who came to kill you?" Jonah sprang up and paced the office, which amused her since it was so small, and he wasn't.

"I don't know how or why, Jonah. All I know is, he did save my life. And according to the latest nightmare, he's trying to do it again."

How long do the blasted painkillers take?

Jonah ran one hand through his thick, dark hair. "I don't know either, Addie. Of course it matters. And I thank God every day he was there. But how? And why? Those I need answered before I can feel better about him." He slumped back into the chair.

"Agreed."

That brought up his head. "What? Just like that?" he asked with a hint of a smile.

"Yes. I also want to know those things. The way he looked at me, Jonah. It was like he *knew* me. But how could that be?"

Something tickled the dark recesses of her brain. Something she should know but couldn't remember. But her head ached, and she couldn't think clearly.

"I did my best to find out anything about our mystery man. He's pretty much a clean slate." Jonah pulled a small notebook from his back pocket. "Robert William Martin was born on March thirtieth, nineteen sixty-two, in Kent, England, to William and Mary Catherine. He is their only child. Both are now deceased.

"The family moved to the states when Martin was in elementary school. His father was attached to the British Embassy in Washington. Robert attended private schools through high school and graduated summa cum laude from Georgetown University, with a degree in history. He speaks five languages and works for the government, like he said."

"Okay. None of that sounds interesting, but it does explain the faint British accent I heard," Addie said.

"His adult life is also quite vanilla. Lives in a townhome in

Alexandria, Virginia. Never married, no kids. No pets. His credit score is excellent. He doesn't even have so much as a parking ticket."

"Who doesn't get a parking ticket?" Addie groused.

"Exactly," Jonah agreed.

Addie squinted at him, then winced from the pain. "I'm sorry. You lost me."

"Robert Martin is a spy."

"What?" Addie exclaimed. "I know we joked about him 'working for the government in D.C.', but that's all it was. A joke." Now *she* wanted to pace. "And even if you're right, Jonah, what does that have to do with me?"

Back went his hand, raking through his already disheveled hair.

"I wish I knew, Addie. Why would a spy, or whatever he is, know your name? Come looking for you?"

Addie threw up her hands. "I haven't a clue but sure wish I did. I should have just asked him," she muttered.

Jonah laughed. "And how would that conversation have gone? 'Robert, I know you know me, saved me in fact. I don't know how, though. Mind connecting the dots?' Can you imagine asking him that?"

"Well, not when you put it like that. I would have come up with something a bit smoother."

Jonah laughed. "Smoother? Really? You?"

"Hey now, I can be smooth when I want to," she protested weakly.

"Sorry, Addie, you know I love you. And you have a lot of amazing qualities. But smooth isn't one of them. You're practically the queen of nervous blurting."

He's not wrong...

"Do I at least get a crown with that title?" Addie laughed at her own foolishness, relishing these moments in the midst of the other madness. But then Jonah stopped laughing. His brows lowered.

"What?" she asked, not sure if she wanted to know.

"Here's where it gets weird. I found out all that stuff easily, then hit a wall. A high, barbed wire-covered security clearance wall. As in 'I don't have the clearance to find out anything else about him.' And neither does my chief. Which brings us right back to spy."

"And leaves us nowhere, as the connection between me and a 'spy' is unfathomable."

"Yes. So now you can tell me whatever it is you don't care to about Dan."

His dark eyes softened as he took her hand in his.

Addie chewed on her bottom lip. She didn't want to lie to Jonah ever. But she also didn't want to be a liability that held him back.

"Honey, whatever it is can't be that bad. I mean, really. Worse than your stalker?"

Tears built in her eyes, adding to the already almost unbearable pressure in her head.

"I can't live with being the reason something happens to you, Jonah. Either to you personally or to your career. I just can't." Whatever else she meant to say was drowned in a torrent of tears streaming down her face. She buried her head in her hands.

Addie never heard him move, but Jonah picked her up out of the chair as though she was a feather. He cradled her in his arms and then sat, holding her on his lap. She felt the whisper of his lips against her temple.

"You are the most important thing in my world. Period. Let's start there. And we've talked about this, Addie. Yes, something could happen to me. Or to you. But we could also die crossing a street. Right? Or say we went rock climbing. One of us could fall to our deaths."

"You know I'd never go rock climbing, Jonah," Addie muttered into his chest.

"True. My point is life is short and lacks guarantees. You and I both lost a parent young. Neither of us knew that was coming. But even if we did, we wouldn't have loved that person any less."

"True." Addie lifted her eyes to his. "I don't want to even think of a world without you in it, Jonah."

"Exactly!" He stroked one large hand down her back. "So tell me the other part. Why do you think you might damage my career?"

"Well, I didn't think that until Dan mentioned it. He said…"

She stopped speaking at the sight of Jonah's face hardening. His eyes darkened and narrowed.

"What did Dan say to you?" he growled from between clenched jaws. "In fact, please tell me everything he said, start to finish."

And so she did, ending with her concern that Jonah living with her might 'not look good' for him, considering everything that had happened in just a year.

"You don't even like Dan. Nor do I, for that matter. Why would either of us care what he says or thinks?"

Addie pulled back to see him better. "Jonah, he's not wrong. The very first time you met me, you questioned me in connection to a murder."

"The very first time I met you, I thought you were beautiful. And spunky. Telling me not to make you feel old by calling you 'ma'am.'"

"Jonah, I was covered in blood. Clearly, I was *not* beautiful. And even though it's a Southern and polite thing, I still prefer not to be called 'ma'am.'"

"Your clothing and hands were covered in blood. Your

pretty face, bright blue eyes, and wild curls were not. And you were beautiful."

"You still questioned me," she reminded him.

"Because I had to, Addie. You found the body. You were 'covered' in the victim's blood. I was doing what I had to do. Didn't stop me from wanting to rip out Grey's throat when he showed up, all possessive and guard dog-like."

A soft giggle escaped her. "You were jealous of Grey."

"Freely admit it. And some days I'm still jealous of him," he added.

"What? Why?"

"Grey has known you forever, as you guys like to say. He saw the cute little girl on her first day of school. He knew your dreams and fears in high school. I know it's stupid, Addie, but Grey has thirty years' advantage on me."

"True, Jonah. But guess what Grey doesn't have?"

"What?"

"My heart. I love him, and always will. But you own my heart, Jonah." She placed his hand on her chest, covering it with her own. "Only you, Jonah."

Jonah stared at her and swallowed hard.

"Well, speaking of your heart, Addie, I have a question for you."

Jonah smiled into her eyes, and she felt it all the way to her soul. Her heart pounded in her chest, threatening to burst. She nodded because she couldn't speak if her life depended on it.

Just then, a short knock sounded on the door before it burst open. Grey lounged in the doorway.

"Hey, kids, sorry to interrupt. Addie, Mrs. Henry is here and demands to see you. Something about 'that dead chef.' Should I tell her you're busy?"

Noise from outside the door drew their attention. Mrs.

Henry appeared. She glanced at Addie, seated on Jonah's lap in her desk chair, and grinned.

"I can see you're all 'busy,' as Grey said. But I thought you might like to know who bumped off poor Chef Guillaume."

---

14

*A*ddie scrambled off Jonah's lap, even though they weren't doing anything improper.

Grey burst out laughing, but not feeling suicidal, he kept whatever thoughts lurked in his head to himself.

Jonah stood and took a few steps toward the old lady. "Mrs. Henry, great to see you again. Now what's this about knowing who the killer might be?"

Mrs. Henry placed one gnarled hand on his arm. "Well, I'd be pleased to share my information with you, Detective Wolfe, but aren't you off the case? Being at the scene of the crime and all. And before you tell me to talk to Detective Blackwell, don't waste your breath. That man couldn't find his own...well, you know what I mean."

Addie stifled a laugh at the woman's outrageous, but not untrue, statement.

Jonah somehow kept a straight face; probably all those years of being a cop.

"I'm sure Dan would be happy to help. Why don't I drive you there myself?" he said.

Mrs. Henry was having none of that. "The idiot – and I'm

being kind – refused to believe me when that lunatic nurse killed poor Bill Hamilton last year. 'What did you expect for an eighty-eight-year-old man?' That was his only reply. And look how that turned out? Why, if it weren't for Addie, I'd be pushing up the daisies with him."

She's not wrong.

She shuddered, thinking back to Thanksgiving Day last year. She'd gotten to Magnolia Haven in the nick of time to save Mrs. Henry from becoming the second victim of the "Angel of Death," as the press had labeled the rogue nurse. And then Jonah and Grey had arrived just in time to save *her*.

Addie glanced at Jonah, mentally crossing her fingers her next words didn't irritate him. "Can you tell me, Mrs. Henry, who killed the chef?"

"I can, and I will. Jenna Roberts killed him."

Addie searched her memory but couldn't come up with anyone by the name.

"The local food critic?" gasped Grey.

He would know that...

Jonah looked at her. He mouthed, *who's that?* before looking back at Mrs. Henry.

"Ah, could you tell me about your, uh, theory?"

Mrs. Henry heaved a sigh before turning her wheeled walker around and sitting on the seat. "Jenna Roberts wrote the local food column, along with restaurant reviews."

Grey, practically bouncing on his toes, blurted out, "Tell them!"

"Tell us what?" Addie asked. She had no idea.

"Jenna wrote rather scathing reviews sometimes. And she happened to write one of that nature for Le Café du Jardin." Mrs. Henry nodded at Grey, who grinned.

"'Scathing' doesn't even start to describe the review," Grey added. "It was, well, terrible."

Jonah ran a hand through his short, dark hair. "Let me get

this straight. You think this Jenna person killed the chef over a review *she* wrote about *him*? How does that make sense? If anything, he would have motive to kill her."

"Oh, Jonah, you're as bad as Addie." Grey shook his head. "Jenna wrote a damaging review of the café. Chef Guillaume set out to discredit her. And did a fair job of it. Apparently, she'd lied on her resume to get the job. How he knew, I have no idea. And last week, so I hear, Jenna showed up at the café, demanding an apology. Chef blew her off. Said she'd 'gotten what she deserved.' She said the same thing back to him, but in a threatening way."

Grey eyed Jonah. "Now who's the detective?"

Addie bit back a laugh. Theirs was an ongoing battle. "Grey, how do you know all this?" she asked.

"Yes, Grey, who's your source?" Jonah asked.

Grey's face reddened. "I, uh, don't remember."

Addie narrowed her eyes at him before Jonah could react. "The Aunties!"

Grey's face went from red to purple. "No, of course not…"

"And they learned it at the Cut & Curl. I was there the day Mabel told Beatrice and Clementine. You know Mabel's great-niece Marcy waits tables at the café. She told her mother, who told Mabel. And of course, Mabel tells everyone."

Mrs. Henry shook her head and clucked her tongue as if she wasn't also a huge gossip.

Jonah nodded as though he understood when his widened eyes said otherwise. Addie swallowed another laugh. Small town life at its best!

"Uh, Mrs. Henry, thank you for sharing this information. I'll be sure to pass it along to Detective Blackwell." Jonah raised a hand, stopping her from protesting. "I promise he'll look into this lead."

Mrs. Henry nodded and stood up. She crowded Jonah against Addie's desk, leaning into him to stretch up and kiss his cheek. Which was saying a lot, since she barely topped five feet to his over six. She then patted his hand. "Very good, young man."

Grey stepped farther into the already overcrowded office. "Mrs. Henry, may I see you to your car?"

"Yes, you may." She batted her eyelashes at him. "Why, if you weren't young enough to be my great-grandson – and didn't prefer the boys, of course – I might give you a run for your money."

Jonah turned toward Addie his teeth firmly dug into his lower lip. His shoulders shook.

"Goodbye, Mrs. Henry. See you soon," Addie called as the woman left.

She closed her office door. "Now you can let it out, Jonah."

And he did, doubling over laughing until tears streamed down his face.

"She called me 'young man.' Did you hear her?"

Addie nodded, laughing as hard as he did. "How about her hitting on Grey?"

Jonah howled and held up one hand. "Stop. I can't breathe."

Addie grinned. "You're lucky she prefers blonds."

He sank into the chair in front of her desk as Addie took hers. After a few moments, Jonah gathered himself.

"I'll look into that. In fact, I'll make sure the chief is present when I tell Dan. Poison is more likely to have been committed by a female. It's worth considering."

"She was right last year," Addie mentioned.

"Don't remind me." He shook a finger at her. "No going off on your own this time, Addie. I mean it. No questioning people. No sleuthing on your own. Got it?"

"Yes, Jonah, I've got it," Addie agreed on a sigh. "But you have to admit, the food critic angle is interesting."

He stared her down, making Addie wonder if Jonah trusted her to keep their deal. Finally, he stood.

"I better go look into this. Dan has to know about it," he muttered before drawing her up from her seat and into his arms and kissing her. "I'll see you later," Jonah whispered against her lips.

"Let me walk you out."

Jonah said goodbye to Grey, and after one lingering look at her, he left the store.

Grey fanned a hand in front of his face. "Wow, is it hot in here, or what?"

"Funny."

Addie wandered the store for a few minutes, stopping to see if anyone needed anything. All the while, thoughts raced through her mind.

Did the food critic murder Chef? Was it that simple?

Satisfied no one needed her, Addie headed back up to the front. The girls crowded around her legs, smiling at her and edging closer for a pat on the head or belly rub. She crouched down, crooning to them and petting both. After slipping them a treat each, Addie straightened up and turned toward the store. And found Grey waiting for her.

"Go ahead," she suggested. "You look like you might have a thousand things to say."

Grey struck a pose, one hand on his hip. "Oh, I do. Now that we know Jenna killed Chef, what are we going to do about it?"

Addie bit back a smile. The last thing her friend needed was encouragement.

"*We* aren't going to do a thing." She held up a finger in his face. "Not. One. Thing."

Grey's handsome face fell. "But Addie…"

"No, Grey, just no. I promised Jonah. I gave my word I'd stay out of this. There have been too many close calls. Too many narrowly avoided disasters. So, no."

Grey full-on pouted. "But Addie, what if Detective Doofus doesn't take Mrs. Henry seriously?"

Addie smiled. Grey had a never-ending list of nicknames for Dan.

"Jonah plans to tell Dan with their chief present. Dan will be held accountable that way." She shrugged. "It's the best he can do under the circumstances."

Grey dropped his weight onto his elbows on the counter between them. "I suppose."

Addie giggled. She couldn't help it. "Try to remember you're pushing thirty-five, not three. If you could only see your own face right now. That pout is classic Grey. As in 'someone stole my favorite toy' Grey."

He laughed, as she hoped he would. "Oh, like in first grade when Billy Ivers pushed me off the teeter totter instead of waiting for his turn."

"Yes, exactly." She waited for his next move. Addie knew Grey, and the ridiculous workings of his mind, as well as she knew her own. There would be a next move.

She didn't have to wait long.

"Okay, Jonah takes care of the chef business, leaving you and I to figure out and stop your stalker."

"Uh, Grey…"

"And with any other spare time, we need to figure out who Robert Martin really is. And more importantly, what he's hiding?"

Addie shook her head. It was all she could do. Stopping Grey, or even changing his mind, was like slowing a runaway train. With your bare hands. The best she could do was go along for the ride and hope to keep him from running off the rails.

"I'll take another look at your ever-growing list. See if I have anyone to add." She stuck out her tongue at him. "More likely, I'll be removing people."

"That leaves Robert Martin for me." Grey rubbed his hands together, smiling. "You know how much I love a good mystery."

Addie nodded, knowing there was nothing left for her to say. Grey was like a pit bull when he set his mind to something. He still swore the missing Spanish fortune in gold lay buried somewhere nearby.

She closed her eyes and sent a silent plea into the universe for patience. She'd need it.

"I wonder what the Aunties might be able to dig up on our British friend," Grey added, with a touch too much glee in his voice.

Addie sighed. There wasn't enough patience in the universe for this.

15

*B*efore Addie could even start to explain why Grey's idea was terrible, in marched the Aunties in a cloud of floral scent and indignation. Lavender for Clementine. Rose water for Beatrice.

"Young lady, why must I always hear of your goings on from that Mabel?" Aunt Clementine asked, with an edge to her voice.

"Agreed, sister," chimed in Aunt Beatrice. "You know how she lives to trump us, Adelaide."

And now Addie knew how much trouble she was in. They only called her "Adelaide" in that instance. But before she could step into the fray, Grey did.

"Now, ladies, Addie only meant to protect you. Her heart was in the right place," he all but crooned to them.

"Well, of course she did," blustered Clementine before fixing Addie to the spot with a steely glance. "However, you'd do well to remember we are neither old nor feeble-minded."

Clementine patted Grey's cheek, much as she'd done for the past thirty years.

Addie tried not to grind her teeth. She loved her aunties

and owed them everything. But they treated her like she was still a child and seemed to think she was helpless without them. Bless Grey, though. He'd always had a way of dealing with them. Ever since he was single digits.

"Do we think Jenna the food critic killed that poor man?" Beatrice asked, not to be outdone by her sister. "Although he was a snooty person who thought his you-know-what didn't stink, he didn't deserve to be murdered."

"Sister and I heard that food critic killed him," Beatrice added. "Does Jonah know about this?"

Addie glanced around the room, grateful her customers stood out of earshot.

"We don't know that Jenna killed him, Aunt Beatrice. All we know is what Mrs. Henry told us about their heated disagreement."

Clementine harrumphed. "Well, I'm sure she heard it from that busybody Mabel. Just because her second cousin once removed works, or worked, at the café, she thinks she knows everything."

Addie swallowed a laugh.

"I believe it was her great niece, Marcy," she added.

Clementine threw a hand in the air. "Whatever! What I want to know is, why does Mabel always have the scoop when you're shacked up with a police detective? Fat lot of good it does us."

Addie took a deep breath to remember how much she loved her great aunt.

"Jonah and I are living together, not 'shacked up,' as you put it. And it's not Jonah's job to keep either of you in the loop."

"Especially since Jonah can't even take an active role in this investigation, seeing as how he was there and all when it happened," Grey chimed in.

Not helpful...

Beatrice gasped. "They don't think he had anything to do with it, do they?"

Clementine weighed in. "Don't be ridiculous, sister. It's procedural. Like on *Law & Order.*"

Everyone in her world needed to stop watching crime dramas.

Beatrice turned a thoughtful glance on Addie. "Do they suspect you, dear?"

"Please stop this conversation right now." Addie glanced around once again to check where her customers were. "Jonah and I both gave statements, as we were indeed the last to see the chef."

"Alive," Grey added.

"Not helpful," she muttered in his direction. "We are not suspects. We are not in any way connected other than having taken the class right before he died. However, Jonah cannot be involved officially because of these circumstances."

Clementine stood a little straighter and puffed out her chest. "I believe I already mentioned that."

Addie counted to ten in her head.

"Yes, Aunt Clementine, you sure did."

"So maybe watching crime dramas isn't such a bad idea after all," Grey quipped.

"Still not helpful." Addie took a deep, cleansing breath. "The police department will handle this. After all, that's what they do."

"And they've sure gotten good at it," added Beatrice.

"Especially since you started with your woo woo," Grey said.

Really?

"My what?"

"Your woo woo. You know, your psychic dreams or visions or whatever we're calling them this week."

"You had another dream and didn't tell us, Addie?" Clementine shook her head. Just like she did the time in high school when Addie and Grey snuck some of her Blackberry Brandy. "What else aren't you telling us, young lady?"

Before Addie could even address the question, Beatrice took a pointed look at Addie's stomach.

Addie felt the heat creep into her cheeks.

"No, I am *not* pregnant!" she shouted, forgetting where she was.

"Uh, excuse me, I'd like to buy this book."

Addie didn't have to turn around to know to whom the voice belonged. But she did have to turn to ring it up.

"Of course, Pastor William," she said with a huge fake smile plastered on her face.

Addie scanned the book on fly fishing.

"Taking up a new hobby, sir?" she inquired.

Just talk about fishing until he leaves. No need to mention the fact that she yelled she wasn't pregnant.

The pastor, who had to be pushing seventy, nodded. "The missus insists I find a hobby since I'm retiring at the end of the summer. Says she can't have me 'in her hair' all day. So maybe I'll try fishing."

"Sounds like an excellent idea, Pastor." Addie took his money and made change before handing the book to him. "Thank you so much for stopping in, Pastor William. Please say hello to your wife for me."

Pastor William gave her a long look that could have been anything from deciding the fate of her soul to questioning whether or not she really was pregnant. Addie refused to flinch, even though she wanted to curl into a ball and die at the moment.

"I certainly will, Addie." He nodded to the rest of them before turning to leave.

She waited until the door had closed behind him before turning back to the trio.

"And that is why we do not discuss these things. In. My. Store. Now, can y'all please leave and let me finish my day before half of Ocean Grove thinks I'm with child?" she hissed at them.

"Of course, dear," agreed Aunt Beatrice. She bustled over to Addie, kissing her cheek. "You be careful, now. Can't be taking any more risks in your condition."

Addie bit back a groan, not even attempting to correct her aunt.

"You'll come to dinner tonight, Addie. And bring your young man, of course," demanded Clementine. She patted Grey's cheek again. "And yes, you may come as well. I'm making my chicken and biscuits."

"You can count on me," Grey joked and walked the two women to the door while he chatted with them about which of Gertie's pies might be available today at Any Way You Slice It.

"I'll expect you to bring the pies, Addie," Clementine added as a parting shot.

"Of course," she answered the now empty space.

But she smiled at the thought. Because picking up pies for dinner was a normal, lovely thing to do. It didn't involve murder or mayhem, danger, or strange dreams. Picking up two pies, she could handle.

Addie whipped out her phone and texted Jonah, querying his choice of pie for dinner. The added mention of Clementine's famous chicken and biscuits would make his day. Since neither of them had gotten much better in the cooking department, a homemade meal at the Aunties' was always a favorite, no matter what was on the menu.

Her phone buzzed with an incoming text.

"Anything chocolate and Hallelujah!" A series of smiling emojis followed.

Addie grinned and sent a thumbs up back to him.

"Is it too much to hope Gertie has Key Lime?" Grey asked on his way back to the counter.

"Jonah voted for 'anything chocolate.' The Aunties love all the flavors, as do I. If she has Key Lime, go for it."

Grey took out his phone. "I'm calling right now."

She smiled as he chatted with their friend, Gertie. When Grey added an order for a half-dozen of this week's dog biscuit flavor, her heart tugged. Even though he drove her to distraction sometimes – well, many times – she wouldn't trade Grey for all the pie in the world.

"Done! One chocolate cream pie. One Key Lime pie. And I didn't forget the girls. Six peanut butter flavored doggie treats coming up." Grey leaned over the counter and crooned to the girls. "Who loves their Uncle Grey?"

A chorus of woofs answered him.

"See, Addie, the girls love me. And they say dogs are excellent judges of character."

"I love you, too, Grey, as you know. Of course, I also want to strangle you at times. But you know that as well."

"Touchy, touchy. I guess pregnancy isn't agreeing with you," Grey joked.

"Do not start that again, please. I beg of you. That's the last thing Jonah needs to hear. Especially don't joke about it around the Aunties."

"Wait, why not? I though Jonah wanted kids?"

"He does. We've discussed it. But we just moved in together, Grey. Let's not add any pressure to him."

Grey sighed. "Fine. I won't mention it around Jonah." He grinned at her stern look. "Or the Aunties. Take all of a guy's fun, why don't you?"

"Thank you. Now why don't you see what you can find

out about our Robert Martin? If that's even his name," Addie suggested.

"Good idea," Grey agreed. He then tilted his head in that way he always did when a thought occurred to him. "Hmm… speaking of our mystery Brit, riddle me this, Addie. If he was on his way back to D.C., then why did he appear in your latest dream?"

16

*G*rey's question continued to nag Addie as he pulled into the driveway of the Victorian she'd grown up in.

Why would Robert Martin be trying to rescue me in a scene from my dream that hasn't yet unfolded if he were already back in D.C.?

A snicker from Grey drew her back to the present. She looked up to see Jonah's car already there and empty.

"You know what this means," he snorted.

"Yes, I do. At this very moment, they're grilling Jonah about his 'intentions.' Great! We should probably go in and rescue him."

"Nah, give them a minute. Maybe he'll speed up his proposal if they interrogate him a bit."

"Not you, too?" Addie groaned.

"Well, my dear, your eggs aren't getting any younger." Grey lifted a hand to his ear. "Yep, I hear them crumbling."

Addie slapped his shoulder before getting out of his car. "Funny, funny."

She released the girls from their harnesses in the back

seat. Two furry bodies made a beeline for the door. The girls knew where they were. More importantly, they knew the Aunties always had treats. Addie made sure to walk them, and herself of course, after meals here.

"Remember, not a word," she called over her shoulder to Grey. She then crossed her fingers. With stuff like this, Grey was about as dependable as a toddler.

The front door opened before she could get to it. Jonah, tie off and sleeves rolled up, greeted her with a hug. "Whew. I think Clementine was about to ask about my preference in underwear. Again."

Addie stretched up to kiss him. "I cringed when I saw your car here before us. You could have waited in yours, you know. Just saying."

Jonah crouched down to rub the girls' heads. "I'm a big, bad detective. I can handle two little old ladies." The words were still hanging in the air when he glanced around, as if afraid they might hear him.

"Yeah, big and bad. That's for sure," snarked Grey.

"Easy for you to say. I don't hear them grilling you about your 'intentions.' And then there's the frightful conversations we've had about my sperm count." Jonah shuddered.

"You never know," Grey said. "I am, after all, the back-up plan."

He walked into the house before Jonah could react.

"Does he really not know how not funny that is?" Jonah asked.

"Oh, he's well aware. But he also knows how much it rankles you. Come on. Homecooked food cures everything." She held up two distinct purple boxes from the bakery. "Not to mention pie!"

"Now you're talking."

Jonah reached out to take them from her, but Addie danced out of his reach.

"Nice try, Mister," she scolded and led the way into the kitchen.

"It's about time," Clementine drawled from the stove. "This chicken and biscuits isn't going to eat itself. And you know it has to be served at just the right time. It can't sit around cooling, waiting for y'all to show up."

"Sorry, Aunt Clementine. Grey and I had a few last-minute customers. People are stocking up on beach reads already."

Clementine stopped Jonah's progress to his seat with a raised hand. "You know the rules, young man."

Addie knew Jonah hadn't forgotten to wash his hands. He liked to tease her aunts by "testing" them, as he put it.

"Yes, ma'am," he replied.

He and Addie headed for the downstairs powder room, while Grey loped up the stairs to another bathroom. Another of their many rules was not washing your hands in the kitchen sink.

Jonah pulled the door shut behind them, trapping Addie against himself and it in the tiny room. He kissed her briefly but thoroughly.

"That makes this day bearable."

"And I thought you were just here for the chicken and biscuits," Addie joked.

"Of course not. I also came for Gertie's pie."

"Keep that up, and I'll throw you to the wolves. Or in this case, the Aunties." Addie washed her hands and left the bathroom, her half-hearted threat floating in the air between them.

"Your lipstick is askew," Grey commented as they took their seats. "Funny how that always happens in the powder room."

Aunt Beatrice made a noise under her breath before fixing Grey with a stare. "A gentleman wouldn't mention such things, young man. Would you care for some salad?"

Grey accepted the offered bowl, smartly resisting the retort Addie could all but see swirling through his brain.

Addie helped herself to the various offerings, hopeful things had settled down. A nice dinner and few moments of peace were just what she needed.

"Jonah, have you given any thought to making an honest woman of Adelaide?" Clementine asked, as though she was commenting on the weather.

To his credit, Jonah didn't choke on the sip of sweet tea he'd just taken. He set down his glass and wiped his mouth on the linen napkin before answering.

"Yes, ma'am. I have. Addie knows how I feel about her."

Addie bit back a smile at the look on Clementine's face. Used to getting her way, her face colored. Jonah was sweet to them, and always respectful. But he was no pushover. She mentally fist-bumped him.

"I see," Clementine responded before taking another bite of her food.

Addie squeezed his knee under the table.

"Jonah, is there anything you can tell us about the investigation?" Grey asked in a rare moment of playing nice.

"Not much new. We did take Mrs. Henry's suggestion seriously, considering the nature and timing of the food critic's threat. Now it's a matter of finding her."

"In the wind, eh?" asked Aunt Beatrice. She nodded, as if that explained everything. "Obviously, she had something to hide."

"Let's not jump to conclusions," Addie suggested before taking another bite of her dinner.

"You might even consider leaving the police work to, oh, I don't know, the police," Jonah commented. "Clementine, your chicken and biscuits are amazing, as always."

Addie's heart gave a funny little patter. Jonah had accepted her odd little family as his own.

"Thank you, Jonah. The recipe is an old family one, guarded for generations." She smiled at him from the head of the table. "Don't think I've forgotten our other conversation, dear."

Jonah grinned at her. "No, ma'am."

"Sadly, I haven't unearthed anything further on our mystery man," Grey added.

And his time for being reasonable had ended. Addie sighed, awaiting the inevitable fallout.

"What mystery man?" enquired Aunt Beatrice. "Oh, I so love a good mystery."

"Is this something to give us a scoop on Mable? Please say it is," Clementine implored.

And there it is...

Jonah glanced at Grey, then Addie. "We're talking about Robert Martin, right?" he clarified.

Grey nodded. "Do we have another mystery man at the moment?"

"Did you think you could come up with more than I was able to, given that I have access to federal databases?"

Grey, far from insulted, seemed to take the question as a challenge. "Well, not to brag, but I am a multimillionaire. Has to count for something."

Addie turned her head from one to the other. "Now, boys, no need to get competitive," she advised.

"Maybe they should whip 'em out and measure," Aunt Beatrice cackled.

Please don't give Grey any more ideas...

"That won't be necessary. Because we're all grown-ups here, right?" Addie glanced at both men.

"Can't speak for him, but I am," joked Jonah. "No need for a ruler."

"He's just afraid, but I can live with that. All I was saying is that the Waverly family, and me by extension, has some pretty big resources behind it. I thought maybe I could dig up something. Maybe shed a little light."

"And I appreciate it, Grey, as does Jonah. It was worth a shot."

"Speaking of shedding some light, maybe y'all could fill me and Beatrice in on whatever this is," complained Aunt Clementine.

Knowing it was inevitable at this point, Addie did. She explained the mystery man and his odd role in her prophetic dreams. She ended with the latest one in which he'd appeared.

Silence reigned for a moment. Only a moment.

"But if he's returned to D.C., then how does he appear in your latest vision?" demanded Aunt Clementine.

"That's what I asked," announced Grey, with more than a touch of triumph in his voice.

A heated debate started, with both aunts and Grey arguing possible scenarios back and forth. None of them seemed to notice, or care, that Addie and Jonah refrained from the conversation.

She turned to him. "Are you sure you want to join this madness?" she joked.

Jonah took her hand and kissed the palm. "Too late. You're stuck with me."

"No place I'd rather be."

They sat and watched the growing debate about what role the mysterious Robert Martin might, or might not, play in Addie's life. She smiled as the suggestions grew outrageous. But the whole idea gave her pause. Somehow, this man was connected to her. She had no idea how. Or why. But he'd appeared in her dreams last summer and ultimately saved her from a horrific death in the abandoned warehouse.

And now, almost a whole year later, he'd returned, both in her dreams and in the flesh, so to speak.

Why?

After a few minutes, Jonah stood. "All this talk has worked up an appetite for pie," he exclaimed.

Addie rose and helped him clear the dishes. The Aunties had a rule. Whoever cooked did not do dishes. She pointed her chin at Grey, mutely suggesting he help. A few minutes away from her aunts might help calm things down again.

He grinned before joining her with his dirty dishes.

"Please do not whip them any further into a frenzy tonight. I could use a little peace," Addie pleaded.

"Got their minds off your eggs, though, didn't it?"

Jonah winced next to her but continued rinsing dishes before stacking them in the dishwasher. "He has a point," he offered.

Addie sighed. "Great! Those are my choices? My aging eggs or mystery man?"

"There's always my personal favorite, the old when Jonah might get around to 'putting a ring on it.'"

Grey laughed at his own joke, leaving Addie to grimace on Jonah's behalf.

"Jonah, you know that's all on them, right? That I don't have any need to pressure you into something. I, uh…" She stopped talking, not sure what to say and not wanting to make matters worse.

Jonah merely smiled at her.

"Of course I do, honey. Your family is, well, a bit challenging at times."

"Some might say stubborn," Addie replied.

"It's all good. I can be stubborn, too." He kissed her forehead. "Now, why don't we have some pie? I'd like to get home at a decent hour. I still have some stuff to take care of for work."

"That I can do. Chocolate pie coming up!"

Addie grabbed the two pie boxes, while Grey gathered dishes and forks. She thought about her crazy family always hinting to Jonah about proposing to her and was thankful he seemed to take it in stride. She wanted to marry him, of course, and she knew he felt the same. She could wait. A feeling of peace settled over her as she placed the pies on the table. Things would be fine.

But before she could ask who wanted which type of pie, Clementine pounded her fist on the table.

"Beatrice and I have decided your Robert Martin has not left Ocean Grove. He only said so to throw you off his scent. So, sister and I will find him. How hard could it be?"

"That went well," Addie said on a sigh as Jonah drove them home from dinner.

She rubbed her overly full stomach. *That second piece of pie might have been a bad idea.* Her waistband agreed.

"Sure, if by 'well' you mean your aunts are out of control. Again. As usual."

Jonah remained focused on the road, but Addie could see the smallest hint of a smile tugging at the corners of his handsome mouth.

"I know they're a bit, well, much. Try being a teenager in that house." Memories whipped through her mind of her aunts taking a little too much interest in her life.

Nothing new there.

"But did they quiz your high school dates about their sperm count or choice in underwear?"

"Well, no, of course not. Besides, there weren't many dates to interrogate. There was pretty much just Grey. And, as you know, he was never a 'date.' They were actually tougher on him and the whole idea of his being homosexual."

"We'll get back to your lack of dates in a moment. Did they have an issue with it? With Grey?"

Addie laughed at the ridiculous question.

"Goodness, no! Our funny little family, which has always included Grey for as long as I can remember, never cared about things like that. Grey was just Grey. No more, no less. They only cared in terms of his lack of appropriateness as a suitor for me."

"Except as a back-up plan, of course," Jonah added.

"Well, of course."

He turned into their driveway. After shutting off the engine, Jonah turned in his seat to face her.

"Now, tell me how you didn't have dates in high school."

She could feel heat bloom in her cheeks under his direct gaze.

"I, uh, always had my face buried in a book. You know, back in the days before reading apps. I literally had my face in a book. And the high school years were not my best. I was chunky, even more than now, and shy. Grey, my aunts, and books were about the extent of my social circle."

Jonah tilted her face up to his with one finger under her chin. "You are *not* chunky. You have curves, as a real woman should. Heroin chic leaves me cold." He emphasized his words with a searing kiss.

Lily and Gracey yipped from the back seat.

"See, even the girls agree."

Addie sighed. "Oh, I'm definitely 'curvy.' I was even more so back then. But I was always on the shy side. And then there was Grey."

"What about Grey?" Jonah asked.

"Grey and I have been connected at the hip since we were in diapers. In fact, I can't even remember meeting him. He was just always there. And sometimes that made things tough."

"Because he's gay?"

"Yes, sometimes. Ocean Grove is a small, Southern town. Ideas and mindsets change at the speed of a glacier. But it was more than that. Most little girls don't have a best friend who's a boy. And we were so tight. No one and nothing could come between us. Not everyone got it."

"You mean like Tiffany?" Jonah asked.

Addie's lip curled at the mention of her arch enemy from high school.

"You remember her name?"

"I remember finding you after you broke up with Noah in her restaurant," Jonah joked. "It wasn't pretty. And that was a LOT of ice cream."

Addie grinned. "If memory serves, you helped with the ice cream. And that teenage waitress on roller skates thought you were the reason for needing ice cream."

Jonah returned her grin. "True. But you defended my honor. I think you might have already liked me a little by then. At least enough to get rid of what's his name."

"Noah and I wouldn't have lasted, with or without you. He was too, uh, something. He wasn't right for me."

"Maybe because he'd been your *doctor?* I always found that sketchy. Still not one hundred percent sure he isn't your stalker."

"The point is, he took me to the worst possible place for lunch that day." Addie laughed. "Although, in hindsight, the look on Tiffany's face watching me, a nobody, dump a doctor might have been worth it."

Another series of yips from the back seat caught their attention.

"I think the girls are ready for bed," Addie joked.

"I know I am," Jonah leered.

THE NEXT MORNING, ADDIE BUSIED HERSELF PUTTING OUT NEW stock, a task Grey never enjoyed. She loved it. Besides, keeping busy meant keeping her mind occupied and, hopefully, off everything happening around her.

"Excuse me, can you help me find something?" a young woman asked Addie.

"Of course. How may I help you?"

Addie listened as her customer discussed a book she'd read about online. Addie knew the book, which happened to be written by a local author, and led the woman to the section devoted to these authors, giving her suggestions for some of her own favorites. She smiled, reminding the young lady to yell if she needed anything else.

Addie wandered back up front to check on the girls. A smile wreathed her face.

"Someone got lucky last night," Grey joked as she approached him.

She shook her head. No use shushing him. Grey was a force of nature.

"Someone slept for eight hours without any nightmares," she corrected.

"Ah. Not as good, but not bad."

"Hey, I'll take it. Those nightmares leave me shaken for days."

It was the truth. Having Jonah beside her, his large body offering warmth and strength, and sleeping through the night meant everything to her right now. There were too many unanswered questions in her life. Who had murdered the chef? Who stalked her? Would that person escalate further? Who was Robert Martin, really? What did he want from her? The more time passed, the more she doubted his story. But how had he known her name?

"Ugh!"

Addie didn't realize she'd said it aloud until the girls turned their heads. Lily let out a soft woof.

She was losing her mind...

"Sorry, girls. Mommy's losing it."

Addie walked around the counter and tossed a small treat to each of them. Watching them chomp away, she wished for a moment her life was so simple. They had a roof over their heads, love, and a full food bowl. The girls didn't ask for much.

And neither did she, really. Just a simple life with the man she loved and surrounded by her friends and family. Without some crazy stalker lurking in the shadows. And if she could lose the weird dreams, all the better.

"Did I hear you talking to yourself again, young lady?" Grey asked, with his trademark grin in place. "We've talked about this before."

Addie laughed, as she knew he'd intended. "Yes, Grey, we have. I don't know what's wrong with me today." She paced in the small area behind the counter. "I feel so...oh, I don't even know."

"Restless? Crazy? Angry?" Grey threw out as suggestions.

"Yes!" she said, way louder than expected. Addie covered her mouth as her eyes darted around her shop. Luckily, no one seemed to be running from the crazy owner. "Here and now is probably not the best time to discuss this."

"Funny, though." He smirked.

"Sure, because you didn't come off looking crazy."

"True," Grey rounded the counter and enveloped her in a hug. "This too shall pass."

"Really? When?"

"Ah, if only my crystal ball wasn't in the cleaners."

Addie breathed out a sigh. "I want my life back, Grey. Remember when my biggest concern was paying the rent?"

"Yes, and I also remember how much that stressed you out back then. And look," he raised an arm, sweeping it through the air, "you're a success, Addie. Not only is this charming place a staple in Ocean Grove, your online business is booming. And you don't have to worry about the rent anymore. Not that it would have mattered. You know I'd have been happy to help."

"Yes, I know." She hugged him harder. "You're a constant in my life I can depend on, and I'm more than grateful."

"If only I could figure out this other mess, make life better for you."

"That's not your job, Grey. And even Jonah, whose actual job it is, isn't getting anywhere." She straightened, pushing away from him. "I'll be all right. Because I have to be. Otherwise, he wins."

"Ah, excuse me. I'm looking for a, uh, Adelaide Foster."

A college-aged guy holding a long box that screamed "roses" stood beyond the counter. He shifted his weight from foot to foot, waiting for a reply.

"I'm so sorry. I'm Adelaide Foster, although I go by Addie." She glanced at the box, her breakfast threatening to return. "May I help you?"

He grinned. "Oh, good. These are for you." He slid the box across the counter toward her.

Addie took a big step back, without even thinking. "Uh, thank you."

The smile slid from his face. "I thought women loved romantic stuff like this?"

Grey stepped forward, lifting the lid.

The man pushed it back down. "Hey, those are for her, not you. He was awfully specific. Said I had to give them directly to Adelaide Foster. No one else." The man shuffled his feet. "I won't get paid otherwise," he mumbled. "Knew I should have asked for the money up front."

Chilly sweat slid down Addie's spine. She pressed a shaky

hand to her chest in an effort to slow the thundering of her heart.

"H-h-he? W-w-who told you this?"

The young man started to back away, as though he didn't understood what was happening. Before she could stop herself, Addie flipped the lid off the box. And gasped.

A single black rose lay in a bed of tissue paper. A small notecard tied to it with a ribbon drew her eye.

There will be more on your grave.

18

*A*ddie heard Grey open the door and murmur something to Jonah as he let him in the store. At least she assumed it was Jonah. From her position on the sofa, head tucked between her knees to stay conscious, she couldn't be sure.

"Addie, where are you?" Jonah bellowed through the bookstore.

Yep, it's Jonah, coming to the rescue.

Addie giggled at her stupid thought. But considering what had happened, giggling beat vomiting. Or fainting. She lifted one shaky hand to wave at him. She started to raise her head, but the spinning room made her think better of it.

"Over here," she croaked.

Grey had scooped her up and deposited her on the sofa when the darkness edged her vision a few minutes earlier. She'd closed her eyes and concentrated on her breathing but didn't miss the flutter of activity in the store as he ushered out their customers and ensured the delivery guy wasn't one of them. Then there had been the hushed conversation on the phone between Grey and Jonah. Addie sent another prayer into the universe for her best friend.

She felt the rush of air as he dropped to his knees in front of her. More giggles erupted from her.

"If you're planning to propose, I'd rather not be about to pass out," she said.

She then felt his hands in her hair, stroking the curls.

"When I ask you to marry me, Addie, it will *not* be in Smiling Dog Books."

A throat being cleared broke the moment.

"Uh, do you think I could go now?" asked the young delivery man.

Addie sat up, leaning heavily on the arm of the sofa. She watched Jonah get to his feet and swallowed hard. This could get ugly.

"Seeing as how you're the only one who's seen my girlfriend's stalker, I would say no." Jonah strode toward the young guy, whose skin paled by the second.

She had to give the guy credit. He stood a little taller. "Hey, I didn't do anything wrong. I had no idea." His eyes darted to the door. "It's probably best if I go now. Sorry, Ms. Foster. I didn't know."

Jonah closed the gap in three large strides. He pulled out his badge, flashing it in the kid's face, then dragged a chair over in front of him. "Take a seat."

The kid did as asked, crumbling onto the chair. He didn't say a word.

"Stay put," Jonah advised.

He took a few steps away, taking out and talking softly into his phone. After ending the call, he turned back to everyone.

"Dan is on his way."

Grey rolled his eyes but remained silent.

Jonah walked to the counter, pulling on gloves as he went.

Addie watched his lip curl at the sight of the single black rose. He picked up the note. His face hardened before her eyes. Jonah grabbed a plastic evidence bag from his pocket, sliding the note into it before sealing the bag. He then turned back to the "delivery guy."

"Start talking. Tell me everything, and don't even think about lying or leaving anything out."

Addie watched the young man's Adam's apple bob and almost felt sorry for him. Almost.

"All I did was deliver some flowers, man," he whined.

Jonah took one large step toward him, hands fisted at his sides.

"Perhaps I wasn't clear. Someone has terrorized Addie for months. As far as I know, you're that guy. Care to know what the penalty for stalking in North Carolina is?"

She didn't think the guy could get any paler. She was wrong.

He held up both hands, as if in surrender. "My name is Billy, uh, Bill Gentry. I go to school full-time, and I needed some money." He started to put a hand in the cargo pocket of his shorts.

"Stop right there," Jonah commanded. Pulling the guy up from his chair, he performed a thorough search. "Okay, but slowly."

"Sure, man." He gulped. Billy drew a business card from his pocket. "I put these up all around town. I'm a handyman." He handed one to Jonah, his hand shaking. "Uh, am I in trouble?"

"We'll see," Jonah replied as he read the card. "Tell me where you've posted this."

"Pretty much everywhere around town."

"Be specific," Grey growled, earning a look from Jonah.

"He's not wrong," Jonah admitted.

Addie swallowed a chuckle as Jonah avoided Grey's glance while Grey did a small victory dance.

"Where have you *specifically* put these?"

Billy sighed. "Everywhere I could think of, like supermarkets, coffeeshops, the library. I posted it every place that had a bulletin board and would let me. Tuition ain't cheap."

Addie watched as the tension left Jonah's shoulders. *Billy isn't our stalker.*

A banging on the front door drew everyone's attention.

"Oh goodie, Dan's here," Grey muttered under his breath.

Jonah shot Grey a look that went unnoticed before heading to the door.

Addie strained to hear their whispered conversation. She gave up after a moment. Jonah was too professional to say anything loud enough for Billy to hear.

Dan swaggered farther into the room, stopping before Billy. He looked the younger man over. "Looks like you and I will be taking a ride."

Billy's eyes grew even rounder. "Ah, man, I didn't do nothing wrong," he griped.

"We'll be the judge of that," Grey muttered. "At the very least, we need to hear everything about the person who hired you."

Addie's body tensed when Dan took a few steps closer to her. She stood, unwilling to give him the upper hand.

"I see you're in the thick of things again, eh, Addie?"

Before she could answer, Jonah herded Billy toward the door. "Dan, grab the flower box, will you? And put gloves on first."

If Addie hadn't been so close, she wouldn't have seen the hatred that passed through Dan's eyes. The look sent shivers through her already stressed body.

"Sure, Jonah," Dan replied with a tone that didn't match his body language.

Jonah caught her gaze, meaning clear in his dark eyes. She worked up a smile for him, wanting him to know she'd be okay.

She then closed her mouth, biting her tongue, literally, to keep from putting the miserable creep in his place. Jonah could handle Dan. Without so much as a glance toward him, Addie walked on unsteady legs to the counter. She watched as Dan grabbed the delivery box and held her breath until the three left, Billy still complaining about his innocence.

"Well, life is never boring with you," Grey quipped. "Are we reopening?"

Addie nodded and headed for the door, flipping the sign back to "Open."

"What else would I do? These books won't sell themselves."

She walked back behind the counter, assuring the girls with pats to their heads and a few crooned words.

"Since summer seems to already have arrived, why don't we capitalize on it? Maybe change up the décor a bit?"

Addie needed to stay busy, keep her hands and mind occupied. She knew it, Grey knew it.

"Sounds great!" Grey enthused. "I've been thinking we need to add some beach-themed decorations to spice the place up a bit. Play to our strengths, so to speak."

Addie smiled as he rambled about the endless possibilities, only half-listening. Grey truly had a better eye for these things than she. Even Erin did. Decorating had never been her strong suit, although she loved changing the appearance of Smiling Dog Books to match the season or holiday.

"Whatever you want," she told him.

"Really? I can? Even the mural of male bodybuilders wearing nothing but banana hammocks I just mentioned?"

She swung her head, noting his cheeky grin. "I, uh, must have missed that part. And no to the mural. Nice try."

Grey heaved a fake sigh. "Can't blame a guy for trying. But seriously, Addie, how are you? The 'gift' was far from pleasant."

A shudder wracked her body.

"No, no, it wasn't pleasant. I'm holding on because it's all I can do." She shook her head. "Who knows? Maybe this is better." Addie's heart pounded away like a jackhammer, but she continued. "Maybe this will force his hand. Make him slip up."

"And maybe he'll escalate and try to hurt you, Addie."

She rubbed her temples at the thought, one that had crossed her mind far too many times. *How could it not?*

"I'm aware," she grunted before turning away from him.

Addie stomped into the back room. Rooting through a box of new paperbacks, she grabbed a stack of steamy romances. What better to read on the beach? She glanced at the cover of the top book. A beautiful couple shared an impassioned embrace.

"Lucky them." She sighed, carrying the stack to her "steamy" romance section.

Addie then laughed at herself.

Grey joined in. "Not sure what we're laughing about. Care to share?"

Addie placed the new books on a shelf before holding up one on her fist. "Apparently, I've been reduced to envying a fictional couple." Her shoulders drooped. The now familiar post-adrenaline fatigue gripped her.

Grey pried the book from her fingers and snickered. "Can't blame you. He's smoking." He wagged his blond brows at her. "But then so is Detective Hottie. So, why the long face?"

Her cheeks flooded with heat. Grey's boyfriend, Jamie, left last year to follow his "passion." His passion hadn't included Grey.

"I'm sorry. I should have thought first."

"What?" A shadow crossed through his bright blue eyes. If she hadn't been standing so close, she'd have missed it. "Oh, Jamie? Nah, that was nothing."

"Honey, you don't have to do that with me. I know how much he meant to you."

In truth, Grey showed more interest in Jamie than any man he'd ever been involved with. He might not care to admit it, but Jamie had broken his heart.

Grey nodded. "I did get attached. That should teach me," he smirked.

"Oh, Grey. Mr. Right is out there somewhere. I'm sorry Jamie hurt you, but he–"

She stopped at Grey's raised hand.

"If you say, 'is not the only fish in the sea,' I may vomit."

"Never! If you hadn't interrupted, you would have heard me say he was truly the first person, other than me, to whom you've opened your heart."

"True. I know! Ditch the detective, marry me, have my babies, through technology of course." He wrinkled his patrician nose, making her laugh. "We can see the world."

"As tempting as that isn't, no, thanks. I'm kind of attached to 'the detective.' And by the way, that makes you sound like the character from that show *Lucifer*."

"Speaking of hotties…" Grey fanned himself.

"My point is, you have to put yourself out there, Grey. Take a chance on people."

"Easier said than done, Addie. You know my family name, not to mention the millions that come with it, make me a target. I have to choose carefully, which is why I only do one-week stands."

"Except for Jamie," she added in a soft tone.

"Yes, except for Jamie." Grey shook his head, as if to clear it of painful thoughts. Or maybe memories. "Let's get back to decorating for summer, shall we?"

"Yes, we shall. Anything's better than moping about."

But words were easier than actions. Addie threw herself into discussing beach themes, but Dan's words echoed in her mind. She was always "in the thick of it," as he'd said. Despite Jonah's reassurances, Addie worried about the negative affects her "situation" might have on his career. Worse, what if he got tired of living with someone who not only had scary premonitions in dreams, but also had a full-time stalker?

19

*G*etting ready for bed later that night, Addie stared at her reflection in the mirror and groaned. With what little makeup she bothered to wear long gone, the dark circles under her eyes stood out.

Great! As if Jonah needs another reason to leave me.

She blew out a long breath. Jonah was a good man. Not the kind who would leave for such a superficial reason. Of course, the bigger issues were far from superficial.

She turned out the bathroom light on her way to bed.

"There you are," Jonah greeted her from his side of the bed.

She noted the papers spread around him. Jonah had brought work home with him in the past. Having only two detectives in the department meant his work was never really done. And though Jonah tried hard to balance work and life, the sight was far from irregular.

"Here I am," she answered.

The past few days had taken their toll, and Addie smothered a yawn. Not sleeping well, combined with a stalker and the chef's murder, more than explained the bags under her eyes.

Jonah put down the papers in his hand and patted the bed next to him. "What's wrong?"

Addie avoided the question and his searching gaze by getting into bed, fussing with the light covers until they were just so. She then rolled on her side, away from him. A single tear slid down her cheek.

"Oh, you mean besides having a stalker and being involved in yet another suspicious death?"

One large hand appeared in her line of vision. Jonah tugged at her until she rolled to face him.

So much for hiding.

"I know all that, Addie, believe me. What I don't know is why you've barely spoken to me tonight."

His soft question pierced her heart. But what could she say? Addie didn't want to be *that* woman; the one who whined. She and Jonah had already discussed her concerns about her "situation" affecting his job.

"You're barely in the door, Jonah. It's not exactly been all night."

Her argument was weak at best. Even though things at work had delayed Jonah a few hours, he'd still been home in time for a late dinner. He even brought their favorite Mexican food.

Instead of arguing with her or calling her on her bitchiness, Jonah pulled her into his arms, cradling her against his chest. The simple gesture, fraught with love, broke the dam. Hot tears flooded her eyes and the cotton of his T-shirt.

"Shhhh, it's okay," he murmured into her curls. "I'm right here. And I won't let anything happen to you, Addie. I waited a long time for you, honey. No one is taking you away from me."

The thickness of his voice brought on a fresh torrent of tears.

What am I doing to him?

"I know," she answered on a broken whisper.

Instead of sharing her fears, Addie gave herself over to the safety of his embrace. Her eyes grew tired, and she drifted away.

"PLEASE, ADDIE! THERE ISN'T TIME."

A man's hand stretched toward her in the dim light. Addie brushed it away.

"I won't leave Jonah. If you want to help me, then get him outside. I can't carry him on my own. Please!"

The sharp crack of a gunshot sounded from the kitchen. Addie threw herself over Jonah.

"Please, Jonah, wake up. We need to get out of here now."

But Jonah didn't answer her. Nor did he move.

"Please," she begged the man she couldn't quite see. "Please get him out of here. I can't lose him."

"And I can't lose you, Addie. I can only get one of you out of here," he whispered.

"Then take Jonah," she commanded.

Gathering courage born of desperation, Addie sprinted to the swinging door. Maybe if she distracted whoever was in the kitchen long enough, Robert would have enough time to get Jonah to safety. With one last glance back at him, she pushed open the door.

"Oh, it's you!" she cried before everything went black.

"Honey, wake up!"

Jonah's calm voice sounded as though it came from far, far away. Addie shrugged off the lingering terror from her nightmare. She opened her eyes, staring into Jonah's dark chocolate ones mere inches from her face.

He wiped dampened hair from her face. "I've got you, Addie."

Addie threw herself into his arms, reveling in the strength of him. His warmth told her he was okay. She let out a shaky breath.

"Thank goodness," she whispered. And though she knew he thought she responded to his comment, she really gave thanks for his safety.

"Anything new this time?" Jonah asked, referring to the nightmare.

She shook her head, unwilling to say the words that would be a lie. Above and beyond all else, she would keep Jonah safe. If she told him what she saw, and so didn't understand, he could pay the price with his life.

"Huh," he grunted in response, not sounding convinced. He glanced at his phone. "Are you okay? I have to hit the shower and get to work. I have a feeling we're close to finishing up the chef case."

"Go. I'm fine."

One dark brow raised.

"Well, I'm as fine as I can be after one of these. Hey, did you find anything on the note or box?"

She never asked Jonah about ongoing cases, like the chef, knowing doing so would put him in an uncomfortable position. But this concerned her directly, so she made an exception.

"Nothing from the box or note itself. But apparently, black roses aren't all that common. I have Natalie, uh, Officer Burke tracking down places he could have purchased one around Ocean Grove."

Jonah gave her a quick kiss before heading toward the bathroom.

"Why is Officer Burke helping you instead of Dan?"

Addie tried not to wince at the question. She didn't want

to be *that* girlfriend. But how could she not? Natalie Burke was several years younger than Addie, and gorgeous. And also wasn't plagued by prophetic dreams and an escalating stalker. Addie had always gotten the distinct impression the other woman had more than a little crush on Jonah.

He turned back to face her. "Officer Burke is helping me, uh, us out for the moment." Jonah looked like he wanted to say something else, but he flattened his lips instead. "I need to get moving."

Addie's shoulders drooped as she watched him enter their bathroom. Jonah wasn't telling her something. He'd left something out.

Something to do with the lovely Natalie Burke?

No use borrowing trouble, as the Aunties liked to say.

Gracey whined before lifting a paw to scratch at the closed bedroom door. It was enough to drag Addie from her depressing thoughts.

"Yes, girls, I'm a bad mommy. Let me take you out and then get breakfast."

At the last word, both dogs cocked their heads back and forth. They knew exactly what she meant. Addie laughed and headed out of the bedroom. Lily and Gracey raced ahead, prancing in place at the kitchen slider.

"There you go," she said as she let them into her fenced back yard.

While they took care of business and chided a squirrel who'd dared to invade their space, Addie grabbed their bowls and dished out breakfast. After filling their shared water bowl, she let them back in the house. Both dogs ran to their bowls. The sound of crunching filled the kitchen.

The girls had it easy. No worrying about stalkers and strange dreams, murder, and mayhem.

The timer dinged on the coffeemaker. Addie breathed in the rich aroma of this month's flavor, a rich Kona blend from

Hawaii. A coffee of the month subscription had been Grey's gift to Jonah last Christmas. The Aunties, having read some online article about the negative effects of caffeine on fertility, scolded Grey every time coffee entered a conversation. Jonah wasn't allowed to drink it at their home, thus the holiday gift.

Knowing he'd be in a hurry, she poured his, black, into one of the many travel coffee mugs they owned. This one, with a picture of a volcano on it, had come as part of this month's coffee package. She screwed on the cap before pouring herself a cup, adding cream and sugar that would go straight to her hips. After grabbing a bowl of cereal, Addie took a seat at the table.

Jonah entered the kitchen a few moments later. He spied the travel mug, grabbed it, and motioned to her with it.

"Thanks, honey. You know I can't function without my caffeine."

Tortured thoughts, mostly about Jonah and Natalie, slid through her mind. But she refused to send him off to work by starting such a conversation.

"You and me both," she joked, holding up her own steaming mug. "I'm particularly enjoying this month's addition. Doesn't Hawaii sound amazing?"

Jonah's eyes rounded for a moment before his face assumed a neutral expression. "Hawaii? Sure. Who wouldn't love all that sunshine and water? Well, uh, I have to go." He leaned down and kissed her cheek. "You're going to wait for Grey, right?"

"Of course. Have a great day." She waited until he pet the girls and left before adding, "Have fun with Natalie," to the now empty room. Addie slammed down her coffee mug, sloshing some of the hot beverage over the rim and onto her hand. "Great!"

She stalked to the sink to run cold water over her tender

hand. Whining from the floor caught her attention. Lily stood there, ears back, whining low in her throat.

"Sorry, girls," she said in her high-pitched talk to the dogs voice.

Get ahold of yourself, Addie!

Disgusted with herself, Addie left the kitchen to get ready for her day. She trusted Jonah. He would never cheat on her. Whatever was going on with Natalie wasn't personal. She had to believe that…

"Since you couldn't decide, Thai food it is." Grey held up a to-go bag as he entered the store.

"That sounds great," Addie responded.

It didn't matter what he'd chosen. Food tasted like dust today. Despite her best efforts, disturbing thoughts, each worse than the previous, swirled through her brain. She'd choked down half a donut for breakfast before giving up. And when donuts didn't catch her eye…

"If you don't need me anymore, I have a date with some books," Erin said. She then twisted her lips. "And not the good kind."

Addie waved her off. "We should be fine, Erin. Good luck with finals."

"Thanks, Addie. I need to keep my grades up for my scholarship." She waved before grabbing her backpack and leaving.

"Okay, now that your babysitter's gone, talk to me." Grey glanced around the front of the store before placing their lunch on the counter.

"Erin is not my babysitter, Grey. I certainly don't require one at my age," she sniped before walking behind the counter. She gave each of the girls a treat before sliding onto her stool.

"Because I'm your very best friend in the whole world and you're going through a rough time right now, I'll let that snippy tone slide, young lady. But only once." Grey slid his shades to the end of his nose and peered over them at her, making her laugh.

"Oh, Grey, what would I ever do without you?"

"I have no idea. But luckily, you'll never have to find out."

"Let's hope not," she murmured.

"Now, don't think you're getting away with anything. Tell Uncle Grey what's got your panties in a twist." He shook a finger in her face. "I mean besides the mad man stalking you and the chef dying moments after being in your presence. Oh, and let's not forget the terrible nightmares."

Addie sniffed back the threatening tears. "This is worse than all the other stuff combined." She let out a shaky breath. "Jonah is going to leave me."

20

*G*rey burst out laughing. Until he looked more closely at her face. The hot tears welling in her eyes may have given it away. She hadn't been kidding.

"Wait, you're serious?" His blue eyes threatened to pop from his gorgeous face.

Addie nodded, afraid to speak. She'd already let the awful truth out into the universe. She couldn't bear to hear it again.

"Oh, sweetie, no. Just no. Jonah loves you. He plays with the girls, rolling around on the floor and getting covered in dog hair. He hasn't slaughtered the Aunties, despite them pestering him about his sperm count and the ongoing boxers versus briefs debate. Heck, he even puts up with me." He wiped one tear that rolled down her face. "Addie, the man took a bullet for you. Literally!"

And another tear followed.

"Yes, he did. That's my point. He took a bullet for me, and he might have to again someday. Maybe the crazed stalker of mine will actually kill him this time, not just threaten. There's only so much luck in the universe, Grey." Addie put her face in her hands and didn't even bother to stop the torrent of tears. "And now he's working with Natalie Burke. And he won't tell me why. Beautiful, sexy, I-don't-have-a-stalker Natalie. The woman who isn't plagued by horrific dreams that become her reality."

The last few words came out as one long run-on sentence in her misery. Addie stopped to catch a breath. Remembering where she was, she wiped her eyes on her T-shirt (another thing perfect Natalie would never do) and shrugged.

"It doesn't even matter, since he looked dead in my dream," she whispered.

Grey took a step closer and shook her by the arms. And not gently.

"Get ahold of yourself. Jonah loves *you*, not Natalie. And he knew from the very beginning about your, well, baggage."

"Exactly! He knew. We didn't even get the chance to have a 'cute meet,' like in the movies. Did we meet while grabbing for the same caramel latte? No, of course not. We met when I was covered in a dead man's blood. A man Jonah initially thought I might have killed."

"Don't forget the part where you passed out," he added.

"Not funny," she growled through clenched teeth.

"Really? Okay, my bad. The point is, he loves you, in spite of all that. Natalie Burke won't turn his head. And maybe it's a good thing. Maybe Detective Do Nothing is on his way out. Did you ever think of that?"

A mother with two small children stepped up to the counter, saving Addie from answering. She led them to the children's section and pointed out some of her favorite books. Dinosaurs for him, and puppies for her. She handed the young mother a flyer for the toddler story times and turned back to the counter. Grey was busy ringing up a young woman who seemed determined to capture his attention. Poor girl. Addie took a moment to skip into the office and shut her door.

Leaning back in her chair, she closed her eyes while rubbing her temples. It was all too much. The stress of the different circumstances took their toll. Add in her troubled sleep, and she was screwed. On top of all of it, Jonah hadn't texted her yet today.

And now I've become *that* woman.

She wasn't normally so insecure. Jonah loved her. But for how long? How many episodes of her terrifying, prophetic dreams? How many times would her still-unknown stalker threaten before acting? She couldn't let Jonah get hurt, or worse, because of her.

And yet Jonah may as well have been the air she breathed.

No closer to a solution, Addie gave up and left her office. Hiding wouldn't help. Maybe a few hours of Grey's relentless teasing would.

By eight, she was ready to flip the "Open" sign to "Closed." And dump Grey in the ocean. He'd spent the past ninety minutes concocting names, each more outrageous than the last, for the twins she and Jonah were supposedly having.

"At the risk of encouraging you, I am never naming twins Ping and Pong. Nor will I use Sid and Nancy."

"Does this mean Alexander and Alexandra are still in the running?"

"Grey, stop. Now. I am *not* having twins. I am certainly not allowing you to name any children I may or may not have."

Addie threw her hands in the air and walked away. She rubbed her head while walking behind the counter. The girls shimmied around her, vying for attention.

"Oh, my poor babies. Such a long day you've had. Don't worry. We're going home soon."

Two sets of fluffy ears pricked forward at the word "home."

"If you think that's good news, just wait until you taste the new treats Aunt Gertie made for you."

The word "treat" was enough to get both dogs doing a canine happy dance around her.

"That's right, Aunt Gertie gave me a sample of her new honey and salmon recipe. You're in for a real delight."

Lily and Gracey twirled in their unique Sheltie way. A chorus of happy yips broke the quiet of the empty store. Addie smiled for the first time that day. The girls always knew how to cheer her up.

"Where's lover boy?" Grey asked, with a grin.

"Not sure. Probably working late."

Her heart sank as she realized she hadn't heard from him all day. Maybe he and Natalie had a break in the chef case.

Maybe he and Natalie are enjoying a romantic dinner for two...

"I'm going to stay a bit longer, put out more new stock," she said.

"Well, I think we need a pizza. And because I'm that nice, I'll even order pineapple on your half." He wrinkled his nose to let her know how he felt about the combination. "However, I draw the line at eating it."

"Fair enough. I'll be in the back, grabbing some books. Call me when you're ready to eat."

Addie walked away before he could ask any other pointed questions about Jonah she didn't have the heart to answer. She would keep busy. She would not think about Jonah and Natalie alone together, solving crimes. Nor would she think about them sharing ice cream or pasta.

Instead, she gathered up some of her new arrivals. She'd think about summer coming and the increased foot traffic that brought. She had some customers who came into her store every summer while vacationing in Ocean Grove. Yes, she'd think about that, and only that.

Addie lost herself in sifting through which books to display in her "beach read" section. She heard Grey call her name before his head appeared over some boxes.

"There you are! Didn't you hear me calling your name?" he asked.

"Obviously not. You know how I get with new books."

"Yes, I do. They're like catnip to you, even though we're dog people. Anyway, the delivery boy is sick, so I have to go fetch our dinner."

Addie laughed at his tone, one of a little boy pouting.

"Poor baby."

"Poor us, you mean, since I can't leave you here alone," he pointed out. "Come on, I'm hungry."

Addie glanced at the books she'd have to leave and sighed. "I'm tired of being treated like a, well, something that needs protection. Lock the door behind you. I promise not to leave this room until you get back. No one will even know I'm in the shop."

Grey bounced on the balls of his feet. "You know Jonah would kill me if I left you here alone."

"I won't be alone. I have the girls and my cell. I'll be fine."

Grey opened his mouth to protest, but the gurgle of his stomach cut him off, causing them both to laugh.

He extended one hand toward her. "Do you pinky swear?"

Addie laughed but held up her hand, wrapping her pinky around his. "This is so much better than the spitting thing we did as kids. I swear not to leave this room until you get back."

Grey smiled. "It was kind of gross. Okay, I won't be long." He waved a hand at the books she'd strewn over various boxes. "Make sure you clean this up while I'm gone."

"Your wish is my command. Now hurry. I could eat. And that pineapple is going to be oh so yummy."

"You have the palate of a child," he scolded with a grin before leaving.

Addie turned in a small circle to survey the books she'd chosen. She admired their bright, shiny covers. "Yes, you'll do nicely in the display." Her fingers itched to set them out in the store amongst the colorful summertime decorations. But being in the store meant becoming visible to the street and to anyone who might be passing by or worse. She shuddered at the thought. No, better to stay back here in the storeroom and out of sight. Besides, Grey would be back soon with pizza.

She chose her six favorites from the piles and smiled. Her life might be screwed up a bit, okay, more than a bit, but she got to spend it surrounded by books. She made people happy, choosing their next favorite book. Addie breathed in deeply, inhaling the precious scent of new books. Electronic readers may boast convenience, but nothing beat the smell of a book. Despite all the other stuff, she was a lucky woman.

Her phone rang, and her heart leapt to the tune of the great sixties hit, "My Boyfriend's Back," by The Angels. Grey's latest ringtone choice for Jonah. Grey had a lot of time on his hands. But she couldn't even be angry. Jonah was calling. She whipped the phone from her pocket.

"Hey, honey."

"Addie, this is Dan. There's been an accident."

---

*A*ddie stumbled backwards at his words. She could feel the blood drain from her face. She blindly reached out for anything that would hold her up.

"Dan, what do you mean, an accident? And why are you calling me from Jonah's phone?"

"I didn't have your number, so I borrowed Jonah's phone. I'm at the French place. You know, where you guys had your date. Anyway, we've been wrapping up the chef's murder. Jonah asked me to meet him here." He paused. Addie heard only his ragged breathing.

"Dan, what is it?" All she heard was the roaring in her ears.

"When I got here, I found him. Jonah. On the floor. I don't know what happened."

"Surely, you've called for an ambulance," she implored.

"Of course. But I thought you'd want to know."

For one moment, Dan seemed almost human.

"He hasn't moved, Addie, hasn't woken up."

Just like in my dreams...

"I'll be right there," she blurted and ran for her office.

Grabbing her keys, Addie tore back through the storeroom and into the small alley where she'd parked her car.

"Dan, can you hear me?" she cried into the phone before realizing the connection had dropped.

"Adelaide," a voice called from behind her.

Addie spun around to find Robert Martin standing there in the evening gloom.

"Robert, what are you doing here?"

Chills swept across her skin despite the balmy, spring temperature.

Robert said he was going back home.

She backed away from him. "I have mace, and I'm not afraid to use it."

Of course, the weapon in question sat in her purse, locked in the store. Maybe he wouldn't know that. She backed away until her car lay between them.

"I don't know what you want, Robert, but I have to go. Jonah's been hurt."

She hit the key fob to unlock her door, never taking her eyes off him. Her hands shook as she ripped open the driver door.

He took a few steps closer, hands outstretched.

"Don't come near me, Robert, I mean it. I'll hurt you."

"Adelaide, why are you looking at me like that? I would never hurt you. Please, let me explain."

Addie threw her car in reverse. The revving of her engine and screaming of her tires drowned out whatever else he had to say. She backed out, narrowly missing him, and she didn't care. Only Jonah mattered. Everything was coming true. Although Dan didn't say what had happened to him, Addie knew in her heart of hearts she'd find him lying on the floor of the restaurant, like in her vision. She hoped the ambulance beat her there. She wasn't sure if she could handle seeing him so still.

The drive took mere moments. Addie screeched into the lot next door to Café de Jardin. In a moment of déjà vu, she remembered Jonah parking there the night of their date. Something seized in her chest. She wanted more dates. Not bothering to shut off the car, Addie raced across the lot. Outside the door to the French restaurant, she slowed, hesitated, unsure of what to do.

Where's the ambulance?

Glancing around, she found neither that nor any police cars. Surely, someone else would respond to an officer down.

The front door stood slightly ajar, as it had in her dream. If only she didn't know what she'd find inside. But she knew she'd find Jonah lying on the floor near an overturned table. And the knowledge pushed her forward. She would go in. She would find Jonah. She would get help. Breathing in through her nose, Addie crept along the outside wall until she reached the door. The waning light of evening afforded her no help.

Peering through the crack in the door, Addie was met by a deeper darkness. She hit the flashlight app on her phone, shining it on the ground to light her step.

"Jonah?" she whispered as she went.

Flicking her phone around the room, Addie gasped at several overturned tables. The light glinted off a trail of broken shards of glass. She picked her way through them. As she turned to look back in front of her, the circle of light caught on a man's shoe. Jonah's shoe. She fell to her knees, the slice of cut glass barely registering.

"Jonah, I'm here," she whispered.

Addie crawled closer. An overwhelming urge to throw herself down next to him overcame her when she reached him. Instead, she took a breath and reached one clammy, shaking hand toward him.

"Jonah?"

He neither moved nor responded. Tears rolled down her face as she placed two fingers on his neck. Other than watching it on television, Addie had no idea what she was doing. Hoping the overturned table gave them cover, Addie tried again. And then she felt it. The faintest thrum of his pulse under her fingers. She kissed his forehead.

"I need you to hold on, Jonah. Stay with me. You promised you would."

A small scuffling sound came from behind her. Addie whipped her head around to see the outline of a man in the shadows.

Is it Dan? If not, where is he?

"Addie, grab my hand. I can help you," came Robert's voice from the shadows.

She shook her head, clinging to Jonah.

"No, I won't leave him. If you want to help me, then get him outside. Please," she answered Robert. "Jonah, I'm going to get you out of here. Help has to be close. I promise. Please. Stay with me. I need you."

The last few words ended on a sob. She picked up his hand, holding it to her mouth, kissing it. But he didn't move.

"Adelaide, please, I can help. We have to leave right now."

But Robert's pleas fell on deaf ears. She would never, could never, leave Jonah.

"I don't know what you want, Robert, but it isn't safe here. You should go."

"I won't leave you here."

"And I won't leave Jonah," she countered.

The sharp crack of a gunshot exploded from the kitchen. Addie threw herself over Jonah in a last-ditch effort to protect him.

But from what? Or whom?

"We don't have much time, Adelaide, please. Take my hand. Jonah can't help you, but I can."

Robert's hand appeared from the shadows. She clung tighter to Jonah. But Robert was right. They were out of time. With one last kiss brushed upon Jonah's lips, she scooted away from him to peer around the corner of the table. She pulled her head back when the door to the kitchen creaked open.

"Adelaide," Robert hissed. "We have to leave now."

"Yes, you're right. Please take Jonah out of here. I can't lose him."

"And I can't lose you, Adelaide!"

But Addie didn't wait around to debate it. She crept closer to the door. If she could distract whoever was in the kitchen, she might buy Robert enough time to get Jonah out of there.

Without looking back, Addie sprinted the rest of the way, crashing through the swinging door. She slid to a halt, staring at the body of a woman lying on the floor. Blood soaked her white shirt, the crimson contrasting in the bright overhead lights. Dan stood over the body, gun in hand.

"Dan, what have you done?"

"Why, I saved you, Addie. I saved you and Jonah. I'm a hero." He gestured with his gun toward a large knife lying on the floor next to the body. "See? She was going to stab Jonah. I couldn't let that happen."

Bile rose in her throat, threatening to pour out of her. The rich, coppery scent of blood permeated the air. Addie drew in air slowly through her mouth.

"Who is she, Dan? Why did she want to hurt anyone?"

"Her name is Nina Leroux, and she is, or was, the chef's lover. Jilted one, it would seem. She killed him in a crime of passion."

"How do you know this? And what happened to Jonah?" Something wasn't right, but she couldn't put her finger on it. As a seed of doubt sprouted in the recesses of her brain,

Addie struggled to quell her growing fear in an attempt to remember something.

"Jonah and I came across her name in the chef's phone records. Up until a few days before he died, that is. Then we noticed she'd entered the U.S. from Paris two days before he was murdered."

"You still haven't told me what happened to Jonah." Addie forced herself not to glance toward the door. She prayed Robert had gotten Jonah out the front.

"Jonah called me after he left work. Said he saw someone breaking into the café as he drove home. I told him to call it in and I'd meet him here. But Jonah had to be a cowboy. Had to charge in all by himself and save the day. Solve the murder."

The harsh tone of Dan's voice caught her attention. Jonah's mentioning working with Natalie today, instead of Dan, raced through her brain.

Why would Jonah call Dan then when he saw someone break in here?

"That doesn't sound like Jonah."

Dan took a few steps closer to her, so close that Addie could smell alcohol on his breath.

"Maybe you don't know your precious Jonah as well as you think," Dan sneered. "Big, bad Jonah Wolfe comes sweeping in here from the city, all experienced and just full of ideas. Well, who needs him? We did fine without him." Dan moved away, but Addie thought she heard him mutter, "And we will again," under his breath. The words sent icy tendrils of fear racing down her spine. She pretended not to hear that last part.

"So, Nina hurt Jonah before you arrived?" Addie asked him. *If I can just keep him talking...*

"That's what happens when you don't wait for back-up. A puny woman takes you out with a frying pan."

His laugh cut straight to her heart. She pushed down the revulsion.

Think, Addie!

"It's a good thing you came, Dan."

"Isn't it, Addie? This time, I get to be the hero." He leaned in, closing the gap between them. "Maybe I'll get the girl as well this time."

Before she realized his intent, Dan grabbed ahold of her and tried to kiss her.

"Dan, stop! What are you doing?" She wrestled out of his grip and backed up a few steps. But her back hit the counter. "Why isn't the ambulance here already?"

And then Dan's face hardened. A whisper of fear slithered through her brain.

"There isn't going to be any ambulance, Addie. Sadly, I was too late to save my partner's life." He shrugged as though he was discussing baseball statistics. "You win some, you lose some. Too bad I couldn't prevent Nina from killing you."

Addie gasped.

"Jonah isn't dead. He's unconscious, but he has a pulse."

"*Had* a pulse, you mean. By the time I was able to check on him again, sadly, Jonah had succumbed to his injuries." He waved the gun in her face. "I see you're not going to play along, Addie. Oh, well."

"Play along? What do you mean?"

Addie froze as Dan drew on a pair of latex gloves and withdrew another, smaller gun from a holster strapped to his leg.

"Dan, what are you doing?"

The light in his eyes had changed, making him look feral. She slid closer to the swinging door, until Dan pointed the second gun at her. He tilted his head, as though trying to figure out a puzzle.

"This is actually your fault, Addie. Everything was going

well until last summer." He took a step closer to her, his face wreathed in a sick smile. "Then you started all that ruckus, and bodies piled up."

"You're blaming me?" She couldn't stop her voice from raising. "Do you think I wanted those men to come clear across the world after me?"

Dan shook his head. "I have no idea, Addie. What I do know is that you messed up my life. I had an easy job in a beach town I love. Did you know I'm from here, Addie? Born and bred. All I ever wanted was to be a cop. Here. And then I became a detective. And life was great. Not much crime here in Ocean Grove." His eyes narrowed. "Until you, at least. There's something wrong with you, Addie."

She had no idea if Robert had gotten Jonah out. She didn't know if he'd called the police. She did know Dan would kill her if she didn't do something. Now.

"It's simple, really. Nina finished off Jonah and then killed you when you arrived. Sadly, I got here moments too late to save anyone." He leered at her. "Except myself, of course."

"No one will believe this, Dan."

A maniacal grin lit his face, sending another wave of chills across her skin.

"Oh, won't they? I happen to know a thing or two about forensics. After I shoot you and Jonah, I'll make sure to get Nina's DNA and prints all over this gun. My plan is foolproof."

"Let go of her," came an angry male voice from the doorway.

Addie and Dan both turned toward the sound. Her pulse leaped to see Robert standing there, his face darkened with rage.

"Robert, no, he has a gun," she called as the sound of the gun firing exploded next to her.

She dropped to her knees next to Robert. Blood spread

across his shirt. Addie placed her hands on the wound, desperate to do something. Tears flowed down her cheeks.

Robert opened his eyes for a moment. The ghost of a smile flickered across his face. "Adelaide, you look just like your mother," he whispered before losing consciousness.

Stunned, Addie sobbed. She turned to Dan. "Why did you have to shoot him?"

Dan grabbed her arm, pulling her to her feet. He pointed the gun at her head, his eyes empty of all emotion. And everything slowed for Addie. There was only the sound of her own breathing and smell of blood and fear. She felt nothing. Her mind cleared. Her heartbeat settled. Survival mode kicked in. It was up to her to get help for both Jonah and Robert. And she had nothing to lose.

When Dan glanced away from her and toward Robert's still body on the floor, Addie took her chance. Grabbing a huge pot from the stove, she hurled it at his head. Not waiting to see if it knocked him out, Addie sprinted toward the back door of the kitchen. If she could only make it out to the street, surely someone would be in the area to help.

The sound of Dan cursing behind her spurred her on. She'd just opened the door when she felt his hand in her hair, pulling her backwards.

"Where do you think you're going?" he growled.

22

*A*ddie screamed both from pain and terror. She'd been so close to getting away. Her heart sank. Dan would never let her live. She'd never see Jonah again. Robert would die in vain, only wanting to save her.

She swung her fists blindly at him, connecting with his soft belly. The whoosh of air escaping encouraged her. But her confidence was short-lived when the metal of his gun stabbed into her neck.

"You're going to pay for that. No more quick, merciful bullet in the brain for you," Dan screamed in her ear. His spittle struck her face. He pulled her hair harder, drawing her back against him.

Addie closed her eyes. She wouldn't give him the satisfaction of seeing her fear.

"I don't think so!"

A loud *thwack*, followed by Dan's scream, rent the air. He dropped like a stone, dragging Addie with him. She fell on top of him. His gun skittered across the floor. She looked up into Grey's wide blue eyes. He held a bat in his hands.

"Is that…"

"Harper's Louisville Slugger? Why, yes, it is. I don't care for guns, so I keep this in my car for protection." He turned the bat over in his hands. "Always best to buy American, don't you think?"

Laughter bordering on hysteria poured out of Addie. She glanced at her blood-covered hands as she rolled off Dan. Once upright, Addie grabbed the counter for balance.

"Addie, you're bleeding," Grey bellowed.

It was enough to snap her back to reality. "We have to get help. Jonah and Robert need help." She glanced again at her hands. "This isn't my blood."

"I already called nine-one-one on my way here. I told them to send everything they have. I may have yelled, 'Officer down.'"

"Grab something to stop the bleeding. Dan shot Robert in the stomach. There was so much blood. Please help him. I have to see to Jonah."

Addie ran from the kitchen, muttering all the prayers she'd learned as a child and hoping they'd work. She couldn't lose Jonah. She crashed through the swinging door, her eyes taking a moment to adjust to the darkness. Pale moonlight seeped through the blinds, casting the room in an other-worldly pallor.

"Jonah?" she croaked through a parched throat.

Where is he?

"Addie?" came a faint voice from the corner of the room.

She raced to him, pushing her way through overturned chairs and tables. She skidded to a halt at his feet. Jonah sat, half-slumped over, leaning against the wall. He held his head in his hands. Despite that, the sight made her heart soar.

"You're not dead!" she cried. She dropped to her knees next to him. Tears coursed down her face. "I thought you were d-d-dead."

Jonah raised his head. His right eye showed the beginning

of a bruise, but the smile was all him, dimples popping. "You're a sight for sore eyes."

Addie threw her arms around him, wincing when he moaned. "Sorry," she said, drawing back. "Where does it hurt?"

"Might be easier to tell you where it doesn't hurt," he joked. Jonah leaned in, staring into her eyes. A dark shadow passed through his. "Dan told me he'd killed you. That's when I lost it. I had my gun in my hand, Addie. I was going to shoot him." He raised one blood-covered hand as if to stroke her face, then dropped it.

"Oh, Jonah! It takes more than Dan to get rid of me. And don't worry, Grey took care of him. But where is that blood coming from?"

She eased her hands over his head, checking for blood. She found a large goose egg at the back, about the same time he winced. Addie drew away her hands, staring at his blood on them.

"We have to get you some help."

Right on cue, the sound of multiple sirens split the night air.

Jonah managed a small grin. "Sounds like the cavalry might be here. I'm almost afraid to ask, but where's Dan?"

"Probably where I left him; unconscious on the kitchen floor."

"Sounds like there's a story in there somewhere," Jonah joked before wincing.

"You have no idea. There are several stories to be told, but they can wait. You need help. And so does Robert."

"Police!" came a voice as the front door of the café swung open. "Nobody move!"

"Over here," Addie cried. "Hurry! Jonah needs help. And my friend is in the kitchen with a gunshot to his stomach."

Addie cradled Jonah's face in her hands. "I don't care how

young, beautiful, and trouble-free Natalie is. You're mine." She kissed him lightly on the lips to seal the deal.

Jonah squinted at her. "I know I have a head injury and all, but that made no sense whatsoever."

"I'll explain later when I know you're okay. And then you can meet my father."

Anything else Jonah might have said was drowned out by the sound of police and medics pouring into the building. Addie held his hand, refusing to leave his side as they loaded him into the ambulance. It would be a long night. She took great satisfaction in seeing a groggy Dan being led away in handcuffs.

23

_____

*H*ours later, Addie sat in the surgical waiting room. Jonah sat next to her, holding her hand, despite being told he should be in a hospital bed. By Noah, no less. She sighed, thinking about her messy life.

Robert had been in surgery for several hours. A kindly nurse had come out once to update them, also warning them it could take hours. The bullet had cut quite a swath through his abdomen, leaving havoc in its wake. Addie closed her eyes, hoping she'd have more time with the man she now believed was her father.

"I know I have a grade two concussion, but did you tell me Robert is your father?" Jonah asked, eyes closed against the harsh fluorescent lights.

"What?" cried an indignant Grey. He stopped his pacing long enough to pin her to her chair with his stare. "Robert Martin is your father?"

Despite the situation, a smile bloomed across her face.

"I think he might be. Right before losing consciousness, he whispered, 'You look just like your mother.'" Yet another round of tears gathered in her eyes. "What else could he have meant? He's not a friend of the family. I've never met him."

"Unless you count the time where he saved you from the warehouse fire last summer," Grey suggested.

Jonah turned to look at her. "It would explain his protectiveness of you."

"True. But why did he never come forward? Why now?"

The desire to scream nearly overcame her, but she remembered where she was. And what a concussion felt like.

"I guess we have to wait until he wakes up," she added.

"*If* he wakes up," Grey muttered.

"Hush, Grey. No negativity allowed." She twirled an errant curl around her finger.

He has to wake up. She had so many questions for him.

"Sorry." Grey stopped in front of Jonah. "How's your head? Does this mean you're going to start having visions, like our girl? And more importantly, did Dr. Noah treat you well?" His laugh filled the otherwise quiet room.

"Noah didn't treat him. He came down to admit him, which Jonah refused. Noah was very professional," Addie replied.

"Well, except for his 'I knew it' comment," Jonah commented.

Addie winced. "There was that."

Grey plopped down onto the hard chair across from them. "Did you happen to ask if he's been stalking you?"

Addie tried to frown, but after the stress of the past few days, she didn't have the energy.

"No, I did not think to ask him that while I waited to hear Jonah was okay." She blew out a breath. "Besides, he mentioned his engagement, so I think we can rule him out. Again."

One corner of Jonah's mouth lifted. "Go ahead. Tell him the best part."

Grey leaned forward, his foot tapping. "Yes, Addie, tell me the best part."

Addie sighed, knowing the reaction that was coming. "He's engaged to Tiffany."

Three...two...

"No. He. Did. Not."

Addie couldn't help the giggle that erupted from her. Grey's face resembled a cartoon character, eyes bugged, mouth open. She nodded.

Jonah chuckled beside her. "Apparently, Tiffany was there to 'comfort' Noah after Addie dumped him in her restaurant last summer." He wrapped his arms around his abdomen. "Oh, ouch."

"Dan also broke two of Jonah's ribs."

"Well, I broke his skull with my brother's bat." He grinned at Jonah. "You can thank me later."

"First round's on me," Jonah replied.

"Pfff! I hurt that scum and saved Addie. You'd think that was worth more than a round," Grey grumbled.

"You have more money than God," Jonah pointed out.

"Got me there."

Addie stood. "Boys!" she scolded before pacing the small waiting room. "What could be taking so long? This can't be good, right? What if Robert is my father and I never get a chance to ask him all my questions?"

Thoughts of the last time she waited there, while a surgeon dug a bullet out of Jonah's arm, tumbled through her brain. A bullet meant for her. She shuddered and thought of Robert. She'd never had a father. Her whole life, she'd gone without one and stopped asking early on after being discouraged by her mother and great aunts.

"Why am I so afraid of losing something I've never had?" she said aloud. "All these years of never knowing. Not allowing myself to wonder. I love my family. They were all I ever needed. Losing my mother..." She sucked in a sob. "Losing her is still the hardest thing I've ever done. I've only known about Robert for a minute. So how can the thought of losing him hurt this badly?"

Grey tucked her against him before leading her back to the chair she'd vacated moments before. "Everything will be okay, Addie. You'll see."

Jonah wrapped an arm around her shaking shoulders. "We have to believe, Addie, that he'll be okay. I know that's hard, but what else can we do?"

She stared at the wall clock, willing the hands to move faster. When they didn't, she turned back to Jonah.

"What will happen to Dan?"

"Who cares?" growled Grey. "Whatever happens to him is still too good after what he's done."

"Hey, for once, we agree," joked Jonah. "There's more than you know going on with Dan, Addie. Things I can't discuss yet. But he's going down for murder and attempted murder. The other charges coming will add more years than he has left on this Earth."

Addie nodded. She'd given a preliminary statement while they took Jonah to get a CT scan. The chief himself came to the hospital to check on Jonah and Addie.

Grey smirked. "So that's why you worked with Natalie today? Not because you're in love with her and planning on leaving Addie?" His pointed gaze at her brought a wash of heat to Addie's face.

"Grey!"

Jonah shot Grey a look before turning to her. "Tell me you couldn't have possibly thought that? Even for a second." When she ducked her head, instead of answering him, Jonah raised her head with one finger under her chin. "Addie Foster, I love you. I will always love you. And while I like and admire Natalie, she's a friend and co-worker; nothing more, nothing less." He kissed her fingers. "Please tell me you understand this."

"Jonah, I know you're a good man who would never hurt me. But Natalie is beautiful, and her life is, well, uncomplicated. I just thought…"

"Family for Robert Martin?"

Addie jumped up at the voice. She wasn't sure she qualified as "family" but didn't let that stop her.

"That's me. I'm Addie Foster, his daughter." The words brought a warmth to her chest.

"Nice to meet you, although the circumstances could be better." The older woman motioned for Addie to sit and took a seat across from her. "I'm Dr. Shannon. I operated on Mr. Martin."

Jonah shook the woman's hand. "Thank you for everything. How is he?"

"Well, he took a beating for sure. We almost lost him not once, but twice."

Addie's hand flew to her mouth as she gasped. "Oh, no! Is he okay now. Will he be?"

"Mr. Martin has a long road ahead of him. He suffered a tremendous blood loss. The bullet wreaked havoc in his abdomen." A frown marred her face. "It was a hollow point."

Jonah grunted. "Say no more. I've seen the damage they can do."

Addie looked from one to the other. "Can you explain it to me?"

"Basically, the tip of the bullet fragments out, causing more damage along its path. He was shot in the abdomen, affecting his stomach and large intestine." She shook her head. "We had quite a time cleaning all that up. The good news is that we were able to. However, the extreme blood loss means possible damage to vital organs, such as his brain and kidneys. Blood loss equals loss of oxygen. We won't know for sure until he wakes up."

Addie closed her eyes on the news, trying to summon the strength from within to bear this. When she opened her eyes again, Dr. Shannon gave her a small smile.

"The fact that he made it this far is encouraging. Mr. Martin, your father, was in excellent health prior to the shooting, which of course is in his favor." She pulled the cap from her head, wringing it in her hands. "What I can tell you right now is that he has a chance. The next twenty-four to forty-eight hours are critical."

"Can I see him?"

"Not yet. He's still on his way to the intensive care unit. I'd tell you to go home and get some rest, but I have a feeling you won't listen." She grinned at them. "I wouldn't either."

Dr. Shannon stood, as did the others. "I'm on until the morning if you need anything. Give them a little time to get him settled. Someone will come find you."

Addie threw her arms around the other woman. "Thank you so much."

Dr. Shannon nodded. "Of course."

Addie let her go, and the doctor left the waiting room. She sank back into the far from comfortable chair. Now that the worst was over, exhaustion hit her like a ton of bricks. She sat with her elbows on her legs, head dangling.

"Grey, Jonah, you should both go home, like she said. Get some rest."

She felt Jonah take the seat next to her. "I'm not going anywhere."

"Me either," echoed Grey from her other side.

Addie's head flew up. "The girls! Where are the girls?"

Grey met her eyes. "Um, they're still at the store." He stood, digging his keys from his pocket. "I should probably go rescue them."

Jonah laughed, holding his injured ribs. "They might have left a 'gift' for you."

"Not my girls," Addie protested. "However, they are going to be starving."

"I'll go get them and take them to your house, Addie. I'll stay a while to feed and walk them before I come back."

"Please, Grey, go home. We'll be fine. Once I see Robert is okay, or at least fighting, I'll take Jonah home."

"Sure you will," Grey joked. "I'll see you later."

She stood and hugged her friend before watching him leave. Addie sank back onto the chair, resting her head on Jonah's shoulder. She felt his lips touch her hair and a shudder rack through his body.

"When this is over and everyone is safe and healthy, you have to tell me how you could possibly think Natalie could ever mean more to me than you."

Addie turned her face into his chest and sighed.

"Sitting here, with you, I have no idea. Maybe I'll just blame the stress of the situation and seeds of doubt I let Dan plant in my head." She curled her fists at the thought of Jonah's former partner. Just as quickly, she let it go. He couldn't hurt her, or them, anymore.

Jonah wrapped one arm around her, pulling her as close as the uncomfortable chairs allowed. He rested his forehead against hers. "And when your father is recovered, I have an important question to ask him."

The End

ALSO BY KIMBERLEY O'MALLEY

Cozy Mysteries
The Addie Foster Series

Book 1: Death Comes in Threes

Book 2: Dyeing for Change

Book 3: Murder by Numbers

Book 4: Angel of Death

Contemporary Romances
The Windsor Falls Series

Book 1: Coming Home

Book 2: Taking Chances

Book 3: Second Chances

Book 4: Saving Quinn

Book 5: Finding Kat

Book 6: Coming Back

The Palm Harbor Series

Book 1: The One that (Almost) Got Away

ACKNOWLEDGMENTS

I write books because I have stories to tell, characters roaming in my head yelling to be heard. But without readers, what would be the point? I have fabulous readers who keep me going in this crazy time...not just with book sales. These fabulous folks delight me with their questions, comments, support, and endless supply of funny memes.

Rebecca Pau of The Final Wrap is my brilliant cover designer, whom I love so very much. With each cover, I think they can't get any better. Then she dreams up the next one... Thank you for yet another gorgeous cover!

Margie Greenhow, PA extraordinaire, keeps me in line and on track. She nudges, cajoles, and sometimes shoves me into new adventures and undertakings. This time, when the blurb just wouldn't come, she was there to talk me off the ledge. Funny how I can write forty-six thousand words without breaking a sweat but not so much the one hundred thirty-seven word blurb. Thank you!

By the time I get to editing, I have read through the whole thing at least twice. And am sick of it! So, I gladly pass it off, not wanting to even look at it again. I love the little notes each of these fabulous ladies places in amongst their suggestions. Thank you, as always, to Karen Boston and Chelly Hoyle Peeler. You guys have a tough job I would not want.

Molly & Callie, my Shetland Sheepdogs, are the inspiration for Gracey and Lily. They hang out with me while I write, supplying endless fodder for their literary versions' antics. And they never even flinch when I hit the rough spots.

And, always, there's my family! They are at the center of everything I do. This year alone, I have one child, Thing 1, starting college and another, Thing 2, learning to drive. Send Vodka!

HOW TO HELP AN INDIE AUTHOR

Thank you for reading Death by Chocolate. I know you have millions of books to choose from, so thank you for choosing mine.

So, here's one more favor...reviews, reviews, reviews! Even if you didn't fall in love with this book, please take the time to review it on Amazon, Goodreads and/or Book Bub. Reviews are so much more important than you could ever imagine.

ABOUT THE AUTHOR

Kimberley O'Malley is a transplant to Charlotte, North Carolina from the frozen North. She is learning to say y'all but draws the line at sweet tea. Sarcasm is an art form in her world. She writes small town Contemporary Romances and laugh-out-loud Cozy Mysteries. When not writing, she is a full-time nurse and part-time soccer Mom, but not necessarily in that order. She shares her life with an amazing husband of more than 23 years, two teenagers, and two very sweet Shetland Sheepdogs, Molly & Callie.

Are you following me?
Visit my website at www.kimberleyomalley.com or click any of the links below.

To ensure you're up to date with all the shenanigans and news, please sign up for my monthly newsletter.